Insanity Tales

David Daniel

Stacey Longo

Dale T. Phillips

Vlad V.

Ursula Wong

If you purchase this book without a cover you should be aware that this book may be stolen property and reported as "unsold and destroyed" to the publisher. In such case neither the authors nor the publisher have received any payment for this book.

Insanity Tales compilation copyright
©2014 Books & Boos Press
"Memory Unit" and "Scalper" copyright
©2014 David Daniel
"Old Man's Winter" and "Color Him Crazy" copyright
©2014 Stacey Longo
"Jack-o'-Lantern" and "Chupacabra Moon" copyright
©2014 Dale T. Phillips
"The Sleep Artist" copyright ©2014 Vlad Vaslyn
"Dark Water" and "Never Alone" copyright
©2014 Ursula Wong

Books & Boos Press
PO Box 772
Hebron, CT 06248
www.booksandboospress.com

All rights reserved. No part of this product may be reproduced, scanned, or distributed in any printed or electronic form without permission. Please do not participate in piracy of copyrighted materials in violation of the author's rights.

Edited by Stacey Longo

Cover design by Melinda Phillips

Banner design by www.freepik.com

ISBN: 0692297642
ISBN-13: 978-0692297643

An early version of "Old Man's Winter" was first published in *Anthology: Year II: Inner Demons Out*
© 2013 Four Horsemen Press

"Science has not yet taught us if madness is or is not the sublimity of the intelligence."

Edgar Allan Poe

CONTENTS

	Foreword by Jonathan Maberry	i
1	Memory Unit *David Daniel*	1
2	Dark Water *Ursula Wong*	13
3	Jack-o'-Lantern *Dale T. Phillips*	29
4	Old Man's Winter *Stacey Longo*	53
5	Scalper *David Daniel*	67
6	Never Alone *Ursula Wong*	81
7	Chupacabra Moon *Dale T. Phillips*	91
8	Color Him Crazy *Stacey Longo*	111
9	The Sleep Artist *Vlad V.*	121
	About the Authors	173

FOREWORD

This is nuts.

This is insane.

This is absolutely batshit crazy.

Yeah.

Pretty much.

It's a book about insanity. Not one flavor, though. There's something here for everyone's tastes. Five writers. Nine tales. Nothing here that chronicles well-balanced behavior.

Which is the point. After all, this isn't *Sane Tales*.

Why is it, though, that we seem drawn to stories about twisted minds? What compels us to read or watch or listen to tales of aberrant behavior?

For me, it started in 1971 when I met Robert Bloch at a party.

I was thirteen. My middle-school librarian was secretary to a couple of clubs of professional writers. She got permission to bring me along. So over the course of three years I met Ray Bradbury, Harlan Ellison, Richard Matheson, and others. And . . . Robert Bloch.

If you don't know who he is, that probably qualifies you for handicapped plates.

Robert Bloch wrote the novel *Psycho*.

Yeah. That *Psycho*. Published in 1959. The one Alfred Hitchcock made a movie out of a year later. The one that is directly responsible for just about every story since that deals with the dark twists of the mind. Everything from *Halloween* to *Silence of the Lambs* to . . . well . . . to all of it. Bloch labored in the darkness of the human mind and gave birth to something landmark. A novel that explored the darkness within the human heart and human mind. Not a story with vampires or space aliens.

A real story. Inspired by real psychopaths like Ed Gein. Driven by things that happen in our own world.

And that's what makes it so damn scary. This stuff can happen. This stuff *does* happen. This stuff is happening all around us. Jeffrey Dahmer, Ted Bundy, Aileen Wuornos, David Berkowitz, Dennis Rader, Fred and Rose West, and . . .

Well, it's a long list.

And those are just the serial killers.

Psychosis, insanity, psychopathy, sociopathy . . . there are so many ways in which the human mind can turn rancid. So many frequencies to which the unstable personality can tune in to hear dangerous voices. So many colors in the palette with which to render pain and misery.

It's terrifying. It's dreadful.

And in fiction we often blur the lines between the fantasies of a deranged mind and the infinite possibilities of the supernatural and preternatural. Freddy Krueger and Pinhead come to mind. The complex psycho-dynamics of the Lovecraftian mythos. The subtle horrors of a failing mind as chronicled in Shirley Jackson's *The Haunting of Hill House.*

Madness, madness, all around.

Why do we read this stuff?

Why do we secretly root for Hannibal Lecter? Why are we willing to accept the violent excesses of Raymond Reddington in *The Blacklist?* Why were we absolutely compelled to watch Walter White's descent into personal hell in *Breaking Bad?*

Because so many of us have a little bit of madness tucked away in a corner, or chained in a box, or locked in a closet. Our own madness. We may not be willing to take it out or, worse, let it escape, but we know it's there. We appreciate it. We, in a strange way, honor it because the fact that it exists suggests that we are bigger, stronger, more powerful and less predictable than everyone else thinks we are. Like Miranda Lambert says in her just-about-to-be-a-murder-ballad *Gunpowder and Lead,* "you ain't seen me crazy yet." We haven't, but we're cheering her on for when she crosses that line. We love those moments when an oppressed character in a story—a man on the edge, a grieving parent of a murdered child, a bullied kid, an abused woman—switches on the dark light inside their heads. Sometimes crazy is the only way to get things done.

At the same time, we often like to read about the bad, bad guys of fiction because in some way they are our proxy. Sure, we don't actually *want* to go all serial killer on people. But we love to imagine what it would be like to have that much power and, to a degree, that much freedom. The total fuck-it-all freedom of saying that rules and laws do not apply to us. To prove that we are above and beyond the confines of society. To be, however briefly and however artificially through fiction, godlike.

Yeah. We do.

All of us.

Even the ones who don't, won't or can't admit it.

In this volume, David Daniel, Stacey Longo, Dale T. Phillips, Vlad V., and Ursula Wong open a crack in the door, loosen the chains on Pandora's box, and let us glimpse what's inside. They drill a microscope into the heads of their characters and invite us to bend close and take a look at what's inside.

It's dark in there. But there are strange lights that allow us to see the things that move across the landscape of the fractured psyche.

Insanity Tales is a strange and twisted little collection of psychological stories in which not everyone is quite right in the head. How they are damaged, what that damage will mean to them and to the other characters, and how it will hit the reader . . . waits to be seen.

But it's worth the time to read these stories, and to consider them.

To taste them.

To savor the flavors and the colors of madness.
Go ahead, read on.
Go a little crazy.
Turn the page . . .

Jonathan Maberry

New York Times bestselling author of Fall of Night *and* V-Wars

Del Mar, California

September 2014

MEMORY UNIT

David Daniel

More and more I forget. Sometimes, though, like trying to recollect a dream, if I can pull out just one thread, I can begin to see the whole weave. Like the trip we made, you and me. All this time later, and it comes back . . . as though I've never forgotten. Is it the afternoon sunlight slanting in here that's made me remember? Something on the TV just now? A dimly felt longing?

A word comes to me, too.

Moonglow.

It was July. We had been traveling for several weeks, in that little black Nash you had, with the upholstery that'd get so hot. A 1952, I think it was, though it might've been a '53. Or was it a Ford? That part I'm not too sure of. I didn't drive then, so I didn't know cars. You did, though. How you loved to tinker with a motor. Like making music, you said. Every chance you got, it seems, under the hood, fiddling with this, tuning up that, the sleeves of your shirt rolled to the elbow so as not to soil the fine cotton. I loved to watch you, watch the way your strong arms moved. There'd be a cigarette in your lips making a thin little razor of smoke, and you'd squint one eye, looking away and letting your fingers, deep down there in the engine space of the car, do their work. And when you'd hear the sound you wanted, you'd smile and wink at me. After, you'd wipe grease off your hands, and you'd hug me and swing me around and say I was your best girl.

You liked to say you were a salesman, and you were, though I think deep inside you were happier working with tools than selling them. That's where you were most in your true self. But you certainly had the salesman's charm. The way you sold my folks on the idea of a wonderful future that lay ahead for us. Pa was skeptical at first. He'd been dealing with rowdy high school students for years, and young men coming around to spark his daughters, what with my three older sisters to deal with. Still, you won him over. I was seventeen, which I'd wanted to be since I was ten. I wasn't a beauty. But you made me feel pretty.

Pa used to tell that awful joke that a girl should never date a necrophiliac because all he wanted was her body. Boys didn't know what a necrophiliac was, but they laughed just the same, a little afraid not to. Pa was an unpredictable man, and Baptist or not, he liked a nip of whiskey. I think he'd have liked to have a son to do things with. In time, I believe he warmed to you. Ma, however, was taken with you from the first. She confided in me one time, not long after you and I met—she said: That young man is going places. Her exact words. I've forgotten many things in all these years, but I try to hang on to that. And she was right. You *were* going places, and taking me with you.

It was romantic those first weeks after we left. Thrilling, as we traveled west from Richmond, down to North Carolina and across the whole green width of Tennessee, then upriver to St. Louis, through little towns and big towns. We were in no hurry. Our goal was California. Where you said I might get discovered and end up in pictures. It could happen, you said. Sitting on a stool at a drug store counter. Or just walking on a city street. Talent scouts were always searching. I laughed at that. I was plain-looking, and actresses in the pictures were pretty. But inside I hoped it might happen, that you did see something in me that had been in the bud all my girlhood years and maybe would come to bloom like a flower. Now that someone really loved me.

On the TV here in the dayroom the show is another one of those police true story shows that are on every afternoon. *Forensic Files* and *Blood Will Tell*. This one's called *Cold Case Detectives*. We all watch them. They're kind of interesting, though I forget them as soon as I've seen them. What we really like, the others and me, what we wait for, is *Family Feud*, which comes on just before supper. Sometimes it's reruns, with that guy—not the big black man in the nice suit—the other one. The man who kisses everybody. Richard . . . something. Sometimes me and the other folks here think we're watching our own families; our own feuds.

God knows I had mine, growing up in my family, my poor pa and the five of us females getting by on his teacher's pay. It's maybe what turned him so miserly and offish. Especially when I got to be a teenager. Of course, I had to leave Richmond. Richmond was the Old South, and my family wasn't one of those families with a name and money that could pave the way for a girl's future, what with coming-out parties and debutante balls that you'd see in the *Times-Dispatch*. Not that I didn't wish that had been my world, or didn't long to be one of those girls. But my people just weren't those people. I wanted riding lessons when I was small, but Pa laughed. When I wanted to be a nurse, he wouldn't hear of it. He'd say you can't make a silk purse out of a sow's ear. His way of saying I wasn't bright enough, or maybe that we were poor and we'd always stay poor.

But you saw the potential in me. And when you came through town in your Army uniform, just home from Korea, why, I thought that you were the handsomest man I'd ever seen. You turned up at the church picnic and you turned plenty of heads. I was sure you would set sights on one of those prettier girls. You could have, I'm sure. But no.

You wanted me.

And after a few weeks' dating—time enough for my folks to form some opinions—you quietly asked me to go away with you. Said we mustn't tell anyone yet. Said we'd wait and when you'd settled yourself into civilian life, maybe working at one of the aircraft plants, and maybe I was working in pictures, then we'd have the fanciest wedding anyone in Richmond could imagine. Have it in California. In a big church. Invite lots of movie stars. That's what you said, and I believed you.

Here's the nurse with the afternoon pills. They come around between lunch and dinner, when we have free time. That's comical, because all I've *got* is free time. Though when you reach my age, time is a slippery thing. Sometimes I can't remember it passing at all, I just know it has. Funny, they call this the Memory Unit, but people here can't recall much of anything. Me neither. But once in a while things come back to me.

Like how today—was it something on the TV?—brought me back to that Sunday morning in St. Louis with you. Driving by the river. Sixty years, it must be, but once I had that small time and place fixed in my mind, more memories began filling in, front and back, like water seeping into a basement.

I remember your car. I believe it *was* a Ford; black. And the way the river flowed along, smooth and brown as coffee. The air was sweet with a flowery tree scent, though I can't name it. We strolled, and you kissed me, and just on the spur of the moment you called me Moonglow. It was daylight, but that's what you called me. We laughed. Anyway, after several weeks of our "unofficial honeymoon," as you called it, it was just the two of us making our slow way west, stopping in small towns and cities and occasionally settling in at a motor court, and you'd go out and sell those tools you represented.

Carpenter tools, they were, made in Japan, so they weren't expensive. But you had to try to convince people that even though they were made in Japan and didn't cost a lot, they weren't cheap, that the hammers could bang nails and the saws cut wood just as good as the costlier USA-made tools. You'd go out with a hopeful blue gleam in your eyes. But it was a hard sell. In people's minds, Japan was still the enemy. Some days you'd return with a wild elation and I knew you'd been successful. But those days weren't common. Mostly, you didn't get many buyers, and you'd come back to the room frustrated.

But me being alone all day, I was always happy you were home. You'd lie back, smoking, your head in my lap. I loved combing my fingers through your dark, curly hair which smelled sweetly of . . . was it Wildroot? And I'd wash and iron shirts that, no matter how you tried to keep them clean, got spotty. Your trousers sometimes, too. I'd tell you how things were going to work out good. Then you'd turn cheerful again and tell me that when we got to California everything was going to be different. Things would be fine and that I should just believe in you. And for a long time, I did.

I once asked you if you'd teach me to drive, so I could share the driving with you. Between our traveling and your long hours away selling, it seemed all you did was drive. And you did try to teach me. In a dusty parking lot. But I couldn't seem to press the pedals and move that shifter at the right time and it'd get grindy, so you said no more. Even got a tiny bit mad at me. It was your car, you said. In your name. And you needed it for work. I liked how clean you kept it. Traveling made it dusty but you'd wash it, even wash out the inside, and say you wanted it nice for your girl. Your girl. If *that* didn't make me all happy.

Which is how come finding those letters upended me.

I remember the day. It was after St. Louis and our walk by the big river. I was looking for a lipstick that I'd mislaid, a lush plum red that you said I should wear to look nice. You said we'd never know when there were talent scouts around, even though I was mostly just waiting around those run-down little motor court rooms while you worked or while you slept, because the work tired you out so. I loved that plum color and I wanted to put some on, but I couldn't find it. Could it have ended up in the glove box of your car? It was locked. You were sleeping and I didn't want to wake you, so with a bobby pin I picked the lock.

I found a bunch of letters. In different-colored envelopes. On different-colored paper, with a perfume smell, some of them. Letters going back a couple years, others not so long. Sent to post office boxes. They were written to you by women. Women who sounded like they knew you. Some had sent snapshots of themselves. They were pretty. I told myself they must have been old girlfriends—I couldn't think that someone as handsome as you, with that mustache and dark curly hair and bright blue eyes, wouldn't have had girlfriends. I guessed that you hadn't mentioned them because all that was in the past and I was your girl now. Although, compared to them, I was plain. I told myself you'd kept the letters because . . . I forget what I told myself. I couldn't ask you about them because that would have looked like I didn't trust you. I didn't want to push you away. I locked the glove box again. After all, we were in love.

You never mentioned them, either, the letters or the women, and soon I was sure that none of them meant anything to you anymore. In fact once, when we were in a café and the cute waitress was flirting with you, you got angry afterwards, telling me that pretty women were dirty and that you liked me because I was pure. You were sweet. We continued to travel, stopping in small towns while you'd try to sell your tools. I'd iron your shirts and look nice like you told me to. I'd write postcards to my folks back in Richmond, just to let them know that I was happy, that I would make them proud of me, and I would give them to you to mail.

Mr. and Mrs. is how you always registered us at the little hotels where we'd stay. Your common-law wife is what you began to call me. Saying that when we got to California, all that was going to change.

I hoped so. You were so busy, so tired. Out for long stretches of the day and night . . . come back to wherever we were staying, dog-weary, having lugged that big tool chest around. You'd want a shower-bath right away. I'd rub your head and sometimes sing to you. I want to remember the songs, but that part won't come. Love songs, probably. Or lullabies.

I never did become your wife, or a movie star, though I have stayed in California all these many years. I guess at first I was resigned to the idea that the police or someone would catch up to me before long and make me go home. But I suppose I was lucky. I did learn to drive, eventually. I had to. Your prized possession—I'm pretty sure now it *was* a Nash—was in your name. And you were gone. I had my license and my own car for better than forty years. I had to give both up finally, and that was sad, but it was necessary. I would find myself forgetting where I was and where I wanted to be. It's the way my mind works now. Remembering, forgetting, and then remembering again.

I wonder if anyone ever found your big wooden tool chest. That was one of the few fights we had. Rain had leaked through the lid of the chest. All the tools got rusted, you said. A total loss, you said. Stupid Jap tools—no good for anything. I said maybe you could call your company and they could replace them.

"Leave it alone!" you said. Shouted at me. "I'll handle this!" And you dragged that chest—heavy as a foot locker—out of the car trunk. All by yourself, wouldn't let me help. Dragged it down a hard-packed dirt bank and just left it among the cottonwoods by a creek and we drove off, didn't stop 'til . . . Oklahoma City, was it? Amarillo? It's a blur.

Christmastime . . . I remember that. Our first in California. I was so happy. You were working as a car mechanic then. I had a little job at Rexall's. You went out to buy some tinsel for our tiny sad little tree. I never saw you again.

I was going to write you, but I didn't know where. And I wouldn't have wanted my letter to be just another one, like the other girls had sent. I did hear from you once, only just a card, from Casper, Wyoming, which, by the time it caught up to me, was already old. But no call or telegram ever came, and I gradually came to accept that I'd earned my freedom in a way, too, though I won't lie and say that I didn't—maybe still do—carry a tenderness. For I remember what you'd called me on that Sunday morning and on soft nights in that hot late summer of 1955. "Moonglow," and because I know these memories are fated to fade . . . if not today, soon, I . . .

The others stir with excitement. A few of the folks here clap their hands, give out with rusty "Yays!" I pull my mind back. Coming up next is everyone's favorite. *Family Feud*. Sometimes it's the old episodes. Richard what's-his-name.

A program is just wrapping up . . . I've missed most of it, woolgathering. A sad story. Unsolved. How seven young women—girls, really, barely out of their teens some of them, and pretty—went missing over several months. In the South and Midwest this was. Nearly sixty years ago . . . and some detective opened the files up to look at evidence all over again. He's a bald young man with a mustache, not even born when those girls disappeared, and there wasn't much to go on . . . photographs, some bones in a wooden chest . . . but he says he owes something to the families of those girls. All those years have passed. I like that people take their work so seriously . . .

What was I saying? Oh, good, *Family Feud* is on next. And soon supper will be served. Last night we had . . . was it meatloaf?

DARK WATER

Ursula Wong

Vicky's eyes drifted upwards to the dark spire and uneven roofline looming over the palm trees. A chill seized her. The strange building was more suited to a windswept cliff and howling dogs than a vacation island bursting with flowers. She wondered if she had made a mistake in coming.

"We're staying *here*?" Peter gestured with his chin toward the dark towers.

"You said I could pick anyplace I wanted," said Jane. "Besides, spooky is good."

"It doesn't matter," said Vicky, swallowing her unease with a deep breath of salty air. "We're here for some fun. It'll be the four of us, just like back in college."

"The fearsome four," said Emile. He smiled at Vicky.

Vicky avoided his gaze. She couldn't stand even

the slightest intimacy with any man since the rape. It had happened a year ago, and she was still too ashamed to tell anyone. She had stopped sleeping in running shoes, though, and didn't always panic when someone knocked on her door. Nevertheless, the memories were like visits from the devil. She'd tried to transform the rage and frustration into strength. It worked at karate class when she pictured the face covered in a ski mask sneering through the opening at the mouth, and the anger made her strong. It didn't work in the middle of the night when every sound made her jump. Relaxing in the sun with her old friends might help her remember what it was like to be normal.

They entered a lobby of polished wood, a sweeping staircase, and a massive stone fireplace. After registering with a dark-skinned man named Abraham, the friends went upstairs. Vicky waited until the others had disappeared into their rooms. Then she unlocked her door and pushed it open. The room was bright with sunlight. No figures lurked in the corners. She checked that the bathroom and closet were empty. She peeked under the bed. She locked the windows, and then latched the door. She sank into a chair upholstered in yellow roses and rubbed her arms, trying not to be afraid.

A short time later, the friends convened at the bar, where mahogany paneling glowed in the soft light. Abraham appeared out of nowhere and filled four glasses with rum punch the color of begonias. He impaled maraschino cherries on little skewers and added them to the glasses.

"You're the bartender, too?" asked Jane. She

pulled a cherry off a skewer and popped it into her mouth.

"I do everythin'," said Abraham. He had gentle eyes and a wrinkled face. "I been here a long while. Me and da wife started with ole Mr. Talbot when he first built da place."

"This isn't the kind of building you'd expect to see in the tropics," Jane said.

"I s'pose not," said Abraham. "Ole Mr. Talbot built it this way ta remind his new wife of Romania, where she was born. He was older than she was, and I guess he would have done just about anythin' ta make her happy. It use ta be even grander. Had a big lawn and a pool with a stone lion. After da accident, Mr. Talbot's son came back and made da house into an inn. He closed up da pool."

"What accident?" asked Emile. He leaned back and stared at Vicky. She flexed her arm muscles, crossed her legs, and turned away.

"I don't want ta scare you folks off," said Abraham.

Jane leaned forward. "Now you *have* to tell us."

Abraham smiled. "Even though she had everythin' she could want, Mrs. Talbot didn't seem happy. She'd disappear for hours. My wife cleaned house for Mr. Talbot back then. She would see him standing at da window like a statue, waitin' for his wife ta come back, his face red from bein' angry. Then one day, my wife heard him yell, 'Ain't I enough for you?' He ran out of da house. Dey found his body lying near da pool. He had a gun near his hand and a bullet in his heart. Mrs. Talbot's body was floating in da water. She'd been strangled."

"That's so sad," said Jane. Her eyes were shining. Vicky knew her friend was lapping this up.

"Problem is, nobody ever saw Mrs. Talbot with anyone 'cept her husband. People here say she didn't have a lover. Dey say Mr. Talbot killed her for nothin'."

"So there's a pool?" asked Peter. Jane leered at him.

"Mr. Talbot's son couldn't get anyone ta take care of it afterwards, 'cause no one would go near it. Island people say spirits haunt dat pool. He had ta let da jungle take it, 'cause he couldn't do nothin' else with it. Shouldn't be anythin' there now 'cept weeds and dirty water."

When Abraham left to attend to other guests, Jane said, "We have to go find that pool and see if it's really haunted."

"Don't be ridiculous," said Peter. "It's a story made up to entertain the guests."

Vicky shuddered. She already lived with the image of a sneering man in a ski mask. She didn't need any more ghosts in her life.

After breakfast the next morning, the friends walked toward the beach. Along the way, Jane pointed to the remnants of a trail veering into the vegetation. "Where do you think that path goes?" She pushed into the underbrush and disappeared.

"Wait up," said Peter. He pushed after her.

Left alone with Emile, Vicky's heart beat faster. Even though they were friends, and even though she could defend herself, she was uncomfortable being alone with him. Before graduation and the rape, he'd told her he loved her. She had said nothing. He'd thrown a book across the room, shattering a vase. Then he'd stormed out. He had written her a dozen letters since then, apologizing. She hadn't answered him.

"I'm going, too." Vicky stepped into the jungle. A branch snapped against her cheek. Dry palm leaves crunched under her feet, but the air was hot and moist. She swayed around a vine reaching up a tree. The vine moved, and Vicky gasped as a snake retreated into the leaves. Emile's footsteps crackled behind her, and she broke into a run. She leapt over a fallen branch. She glanced back. Emile was running, too. She sprinted between the trees. A leaf touched her cheek and she cried out. Her face dripped with sweat. Finally, she burst into a clearing. Peter and Jane were already there. In a moment, Emile came panting up from behind.

Before them stood a stone patio, a statue of a lion with his head tilted back in a roar, and a pool with water so dark it was almost black. It was rectangular and luxuriously long. A sudden breeze disturbed the surface into sharp brightness.

"This must be it. It's beautiful," said Jane. The four friends gazed at the dark surface.

Peter knelt and dipped his fingers in the water. "There's no algae." He cupped some water in his hand, brought it to his nose, and sniffed. "No odor." He tilted his hand and poured the water back into the pool. The thin stream glistened like tinsel. "It's clear. I bet the tiles at the bottom make it look dark, but the water is clean. Somebody must maintain it."

"With the path overgrown, how could anyone get here?" asked Vicky.

"Maybe there's another path," said Peter.

"I wonder if it's really haunted," said Jane, smiling. "I'm going in."

"Abraham said it was closed," said Peter.

"What, you believe in ghosts now?" Jane laughed as she kicked off her sandals and wiggled out of her shorts.

"Yee-ha," shouted Emile. He tossed off his shirt and jumped in. The water spraying upwards gleamed like crystals. He emerged with a grin. "The water's fine. Come on in. No one will know."

Jane grabbed Peter's hand and pulled him down the steps into the water. Vicky watched her friends, then turned away and stepped out of the sundress covering her swimsuit. She draped it over the lion's head. She went down the steps slowly, clinging to the side, for she couldn't swim.

The water circled Vicky's hips, licking at her lower back. It tickled her legs. Her nipples hardened. She sighed and leaned against the side. Her breasts pushed against the material of her swimsuit. Her hand slipped into the space between her legs. She squeezed her thighs together and enjoyed the thrill. Then Vicky pulled her hand away and glanced at her friends to see if they were watching. Her body hadn't responded to anything sensual since the rape.

What was going on?

Jane squealed as Emile and Peter splashed her. The water danced. Droplets leapt into the air, posing for an instant in the sun before falling back down.

Peter lifted himself to sit on the edge of the pool. Jane ran up the steps, laughing, and rumpled his hair before plopping down beside him. Peter took her hand and kissed it. They got up and walked toward the path leading to the inn, their arms around each other. Vicky realized with a start that her friends had become lovers. She looked at them with envy, wondering if she could ever love someone.

Emile swam to Vicky and draped his arms around her. She gasped at the sudden closeness. She tried to push him away, but found herself folding against him like a piece of paper. The water on his shoulders sparkled. She whimpered as Emile's mouth covered hers.

Emile caressed her back as the water lapped against them. The ghostly image of the man in the ski mask appeared. He had knocked on the door and she had let him inside. She'd known right away that it was a mistake. Vicky could almost feel the tip of the knife toying with her ear. The man had been silent, but the knife had said everything. When Emile moved the straps of her bathing suit off her shoulders and inched it down her body, Vicky remembered her panties being ripped down her legs and how it had hurt. Emile lifted her so she was sitting on the edge of the pool. The man in the ski mask had sneered, and Vicky's life had stopped. Emile entered her and she recalled the interminable minutes: the weight pushing her down, every thrust and grunt, the scent of stale cigarette smoke, the threads in the carpet squirming into her flesh, the sound of Lucy

Ricardo's voice on the TV. In exchange for her life, she had given the man with the sneer a little time; that was all. When it was over, she could live again. All she had to do was wait and pretend it was a dream.

Emile stopped moving. Vicky's buttocks ached from the hard tile. Her legs clenched Emile's waist. A red bite mark blazed on his neck. The scent of musk sharpened the sweet smell of the flowers. She dropped her legs into the water. Emile kissed her. His lips were soft. He climbed up the steps. Scratch lines marked his back. He lay on the warm stone. Vicky covered her breasts with her arms.

Her bathing suit floated on the water as if nothing had happened. She grabbed it and stretched it over her skin. She climbed the stairs, stepped into her sandals, and pulled her dress off the lion. She ran into the jungle. Vicky stopped near the vine with the snake that had slithered into a tree, and vomited into the palm leaves.

That evening, Vicky stared at the door, hoping that the knocking would stop. She opened it when Jane called her name.

"Everybody's waiting for you downstairs," said Jane.

Vicky turned her back to her friend who followed her inside. "I'm not going."

"Why?"

"I'm so ashamed. Emile and I . . ."

"I'm glad you two finally got together."

Vicky covered her face with her hands.

"The first time with someone new is always bad,

but it'll get better. You two were meant for each other." Jane pulled a dress from the closet and handed it to Vicky. "I'm not going down without you."

Vicky reluctantly took off her t-shirt and pulled the dress over her head. She followed Jane down to the veranda like a lost puppy. Peter and Emile were sitting at a table with a bottle of wine and four glasses.

When Vicky sat down, Emile smiled and put his hand over hers. She snatched it away.

"What's wrong?" asked Emile.

Vicky took a gulp of wine. "You shouldn't have done it. I thought we were friends."

"I didn't *make* you do anything," said Emile.

Jane and Peter exchanged glances. "You two want to be alone?" Peter asked.

"What's going on, Vicky?" asked Jane. "I thought it was just the first-time jitters."

"I was raped," said Vicky.

Emile's face turned gray. "I didn't rape you." He looked down at his hands.

"It happened last spring, just before graduation. I was home alone. I let him in. He had a knife, and a ski mask over his face," said Vicky. Her throat burned as if each word had left a trail of fire.

"Did you report it? Did they catch the bastard?" asked Jane.

Vicky shook her head. "I was too ashamed. I vowed never to let a man do that to me again."

"Sex is no big deal," said Peter. "Just forget about it. I would."

"What is wrong with you? Somebody raped her," Jane said.

"Today in the pool, I didn't want to do that," said Vicky.

"I didn't force you into anything," Emile said.

"*Something* did. Something made me do it," said Vicky. Her head pounded.

"If it was a mistake, just say so," Emile said.

"I don't know what happened back there. The water was so beautiful. I wanted to push you away." Vicky shook her head. "It was like the water drew me to you, but that's impossible." Vicky forced the next words out. "Unless the pool *is* haunted, like Abraham said."

"If you don't love me, at least be honest about it, but don't make up ridiculous excuses," said Emile.

"I don't love you. I never have, and I never will." Vicky bumped into the table as she stood. Her glass fell over, the wine bleeding onto the white tablecloth.

"But I've always loved you." Emile's voice drifted out to her as she ran away.

The next morning, Jane's incessant knocking on the door brought Vicky out of a half-sleep of shadows, churning water, and a knife tickling her ear.

"I don't want to see him," said Vicky.

"Emile wouldn't hurt you." Jane pulled shorts and a t-shirt out of the drawer and threw them on the bed. "Come on. He's your friend."

"It was the pool, damn it. And none of you believe me."

"Vicky, that's nonsense. Please just talk to him. The four of us used to have so much fun together.

Don't ruin it."

Vicky dressed and shuffled down to the breakfast room with Jane. Peter was already devouring a plate of fresh fruit and eggs. Vicky felt Emile's gaze on her as he took a puff of a cigarette.

"I thought you gave that up," Vicky said.

Emile pressed the cigarette into an ashtray. A thin curlicue of smoke drifted into the air. "Look, if you think the pool is haunted, let's go there and find out for sure."

Vicky sipped her coffee and nodded. She had to know if the pool had possessed her. She glanced at Emile. She had to face the answer, whatever it was.

They finished breakfast in silence. After changing into their bathing suits, they retraced the path to the isolated clearing. Emile, Jane, and Peter stood on the stone patio next to the roaring lion.

"This is exciting," said Jane.

Vicky gingerly put one foot into the glistening water.

"You don't want us to go in with you, do you?" Peter asked.

Vicky shook her head. She needed to do this alone. She was strong. It was just a pool. There was no reason to be scared. As she went deeper, the water became colder. As it slapped her waist, a sensation of dread filled her, and she had an overwhelming urge to leave.

"Are you horny yet?" asked Peter.

Jane punched him in the arm. "Shut up."

"The water's freezing. I'm getting out," said Vicky.

As she turned, Emile ran to the pool and jumped in, sending a cascade of water up in the air.

The ripples faded away and the water became still.

"He's staying down too long. Is this a joke?" asked Jane. "Are you in on this?"

"No," Peter said. "We're not doing anything."

"He's not coming up!" said Vicky. She forgot that she couldn't swim. She splashed to the spot where she had last seen Emile. Her feet couldn't touch bottom. She thrashed her arms and legs, trying to stay afloat. She took a deep breath and put her face in. Though it was broad daylight, the water was too dark to see anything. She stretched her arms down as far as she could. The water glided past her empty hands.

Vicky lifted her head and took a breath. "Emile!" Something touched her legs. She kicked frantically. She couldn't keep her head up. Water washed over her face. She opened her mouth to scream and liquid rushed in. It invaded her nose and lungs. She sank. Her chest felt like it was going to explode. Then her arms and legs went limp. A sense of calm washed over her.

So this is what it feels like to die.

Then she was being pulled up. Sweet, welcome air rushed into her mouth and nose. Vicky sputtered and gasped against Peter's chest as he carried her out of the pool.

"There's some kind of current in there. I barely saved you." Peter put his hands on his knees and panted.

Jane came up to the surface, her face ashen. "I

can't see anything," she gasped.

"Get the hell out of there," said Peter. "We need to get help!"

Vicky paused, her chest heaving. She pulled herself into the jungle. She stumbled through the undergrowth, ignoring the branches hitting her face, and the sticks cutting her feet. She thought of the cigarette at breakfast and the stink of smoke on the ski mask. Emile had stormed out in anger just before the rape. His touch yesterday had brought her right back to those awful moments when she was pinned down on the carpet. She stopped running. Was it possible? In all those letters, was he apologizing for raping her? Was Emile the one who had shattered her sense of peace, and her ability to trust another person?

She could lose her way in the jungle. Help would arrive, but too late to do any good. She could have her revenge, and no one would ever know.

But she wasn't absolutely sure it was him. They had been friends. She had to save him.

Vicky picked up her stride and pushed on toward the inn, finally slamming the door open and shouting for Abraham.

When Vicky returned to the pool, Emile had surfaced, and was floating facedown in the water. Peter and Jane were pulling him out.

Vicky ran to the body. Emile's lips were blue. His skin was cold. She steeled her stomach, put her lips over his, and breathed into him until medics arrived.

That night, Vicky, Peter, and Jane sat on the

veranda as a light breeze brought them the scent of flowers.

Finally, Vicky broke the silence. "It was because of the water. It seduced us into having sex, and then it killed Emile."

"You've got to stop talking like that," said Peter.

"I'd been raped. I didn't want sex. So why did we do it? And what about you and Jane?" asked Vicky.

"We've known each other for years. It was inevitable that we get together," said Peter.

"Something pulled me under when I tried to save Emile," Vicky said.

"There was a current. Besides, you can't swim. Of course you sank. What's wrong with you?" asked Jane.

"A current in a swimming pool?" Vicky felt sick. If she hadn't said it was haunted, they would never have gone back there. If she hadn't paused on the way to the inn to think about her rapist, help might have arrived in time to save him.

"We were splashing around, trying to find him. That's what you felt," said Peter.

"But why did Emile drown?" asked Vicky.

"He must have hit his head when he went in," said Peter.

"He wasn't near the edge!" Vicky said.

"Stop shouting," said Jane. She covered her ears with her hands.

"Why can't you see what happened?" Vicky grabbed Peter's arm.

"Why couldn't you see that he loved you? He always loved you. He was just never good enough for you," Peter said. He savagely pulled his arm away.

Vicky stood so quickly that her chair fell over with a bang.

"Get a grip. He's dead and that's it," said Peter. He took Jane by the hand, and led her away.

Once the crowd had dispersed, Vicky made her way over the grass to the willow tree blossoming in yellow flowers, and to the coffin that lay beneath it. The sobs from Emile's parents lingered in the air. Peter's and Jane's silence had stung, so Vicky had stood in the back by herself, listening to the eulogy and fighting the urge to cry.

She put her hand on the cool metal surface. The sky reflected perfectly, and it looked like the coffin was full of clouds. Vicky gazed down at the clouds and the yellow flowers hanging from the branches overhead. She saw her face lined with dried tears.

As she leaned in closer, the man in the ski mask appeared before her: his eyes closed, his head resting on the white satin pillow . . . and a sneer, curling on his face.

JACK-O'-LANTERN

Dale T. Phillips

The girl frowned at her parents. "What? Why are we moving?"

"Because we can have our own home there. I'm sure you'll love it, Jackie."

"Mom, I've told you, please don't call me that."

Her mother rolled her eyes. "Well, you won't let us call you Jacqueline. But *Jay* is a boy's name."

"It's *my* name. And I have friends here. I don't want to move."

"You'll make new friends." Her father tousled her hair as if she wasn't fully eleven years old, but simply a little kid, which she hated. *Easy for him,* she thought. *He doesn't have any friends here.* They'd spent the last five years on the coast of Maine so he could pursue his dream of being an artist, but he'd done nothing of note. Instead of being inspired, he'd said he felt uneasy being so near the ocean.

Her mother fake-smiled, the way she did when she was trying to get Jay to do something she didn't want to do, like eat beets. "This is just a rental, and it costs a lot. We can't afford it anymore. The one in Iowa is ours for nothing."

"Who gives away a free house? What's wrong with it?"

"It belonged to Daddy's cousins, dear. They went away years ago, and the estate was finally settled. There are no other relatives, so it goes to your father."

"That's weird. Who just disappears like that?"

"Their son died, so they probably just moved away somewhere else. Bad memories for them, most likely."

Jay gnawed her lip. "What'll we do there?"

"Well, your father can finally paint, and I'll . . . well, I'm sure I'll find something to do."

Not very likely, thought Jay. "What if we don't like it?"

"We'll learn to like it," her father said, his eyes cold. "We're moving, and that's that." He stood up and walked into the other room, his shoulders stiff, the way they got when he was irritated.

Jay watched him go. *He doesn't care. I don't know if he ever did.* The thought made her sad.

"Oh, don't cry, dear," said her mother. "I'm sure you'll like it just fine."

Jay had gotten used to living near the shore, with pretty shells and bits of weathered glass to pick up on her beach walks, and the beautiful rolling ocean, dotted with white-sailed boats. She loved the shape of the mountains she could see from her house.

But when they arrived in Iowa, there were no mountains and no ocean, except for oceans of corn fields. The smells were different, with a decayed tone of ripe earth and stinky pigs from a farm down the road. When there was any wind, it blew hot and clammy, not like the cooling breeze off the water of Penobscot Bay.

Her new home was stuck out in the fields, far away from anything, and certainly looked like it had been abandoned. It seemed lonely out on the flat landscape. Jay hadn't been expecting much, but she was stunned at the state of disrepair. Her father had cheerily pronounced it a 'fixer-upper,' and Jay's heart sank, knowing that he could barely use a hammer without banging his thumb. Her mother wasn't much better.

Though they gave it a half-hearted try for the first two weeks, the repairs they did were cosmetic, and many of the important things were not done by the time Jay started school. Her upstairs bedroom smelled musty, the downstairs bathroom didn't work, and paint peeled on the outside, while wallpaper frayed on the inside. The front door stuck, and so did most of the windows. There were mouse nests everywhere, and they had to spray everything to get large colonies of insects and spiders to vacate. The house really felt like people had suddenly left it, and as a result, it had started to wither away as a home.

And there were the framed photographs on the wall. The people in them looked unhappy and uncomfortable. One was a bald-headed man with round glasses and a big dark birthmark over one eye, who stared straight into the camera. The other was a grim-lipped woman with hair pulled back into a tight bun, who seemed to be looking past the photographer to something else. Jay asked who they were, and was told they were the cousins who had lived there before. *But no picture of their son who died*, thought Jay. It bothered her. If she died, would her parents get rid of all the pictures of her? Walking by the pictures of ghosts made her uneasy every time, but she resolved to make the best of it.

Jay's new school was a saggy old building, looking tired and weathered, like the people, who stared at her like some exotic zoo creature. She got off on the wrong foot the first day of class, when her teacher introduced her.

"Class, this is Jacqueline. That's a pretty name, but I think we'll call her Jackie."

"No ma'am, please don't do that. Please call me Jay."

"*Jay?*" The teacher laughed with a harsh smoker's rasp. "Jay is a *boy's* name. You're not a boy, are you?"

"No, ma'am, I'm a girl, but please call me Jay."

The teacher scrunched up her face like she'd bit into something and found a bug. Jay tried to keep a pleasant expression and gazed back, unwilling to back down. But she could tell the teacher didn't like that.

"Very well," the woman huffed. "Class, it appears as if we have a *tomboy*. Please take your seat, *Jay*."

She almost spat the name.

"Yes ma'am. Thank you, ma'am." *Why can't people let me have my own name?*

At recess, the other kids were merciless, taunting Jay, and yelling *tomboy, tomboy*. She didn't give them a reaction, and most of them stopped after a time, but one fat boy was relentless, calling her names until he wheezed.

Jay finally addressed him. "You know, you're just out of breath because you're so fat."

The other kids came to a shocked stop, as if she'd pulled a gun.

"What did you say?" The boy's face grew cherry red.

"Are you so fat you can't hear, either?"

"You can't talk to me like that," he said, and shot his hands out in a hard push, striking her chest and shoving her backwards.

Jay stepped in closer and smacked him in the nose. He screamed, his hands covering his face, and ran off. She watched him go, knowing there would be trouble, but thinking it had been worth it.

There was trouble indeed, and she sat for what seemed like hours in the principal's office, waiting for her mother to arrive. When her scowling mother finally came out from her talk with the principal, she grabbed Jay's wrist and pulled her out to the car.

"The first day?" Her mother was almost hissing, her face a mask of fury. "You can't even get through the *first day*?"

Jay's lower lip trembled. "Don't you even want to know what happened?"

"I know what happened. They told me. You hit some boy and gave him a bloody nose."

"Because he *pushed* me. He was teasing me, and then he put his hands on me. I wanted to protect myself."

"And *I* wanted us to do well here," her mother said sadly. "I wanted us to have a fresh start, and then, maybe . . ."

Jay saw her mother's eyes grow wet. "I'm sorry, Mom. I didn't start trouble, but the kids were teasing me, and—"

Her mother's jaw clenched. "You told them to call you *Jay*, didn't you?"

"It's my name; why not?"

"Why can't you just accept things, instead of always pushing back?"

Because I don't like some of those things. Jay crossed her arms and looked out the window at the endless fields of green, wishing she was back by the ocean. When they neared home, she saw a dark silhouette against the sky, an upright human figure with arms flung wide. She gasped, recognizing the symbol from her infrequent church lessons. "Mom, is that a Jesus statue?"

Her mother looked at her with furrowed brow, then out the window, in the direction of Jay's gaze. She laughed. Jay hadn't heard her mom laugh in a really long time.

"No, Ja—*Jay*, that's an honest-to-god scarecrow."

"Like in the *Wizard of Oz*?"

"Just so. They put a human-type figure out there to scare the crows away from eating the crops."

"I heard crows are really smart, and can figure out that it's not a real man pretty quick. Can we go see it?"

"Some other time."

Some other time was parent-speak for *never*. Jay sighed and settled back. She would do it herself.

At school the next day, most of the other kids avoided Jay, which suited her just fine. But she noticed a small boy hanging around, and looked him straight in the face. "Why are you following me?" Her voice wasn't unfriendly; she just wanted to know.

"You punched Roger in the nose. That was great. He's always picking on me. My brother told me I should do what you did, but I never had the guts."

She smiled. "Glad to help."

"I'm Arthur. And you're Jay."

She liked it when people said the name she'd chosen without any inflection to it, just as a natural thing.

"How come you're so brave?" Arthur said. "You're like a superhero."

Jay laughed. "No big deal. I just don't like being pushed."

"But you fought him. I could never be that brave."

Jay smiled. "But you're talking to me. Look at all those other kids who are too scared to do that. You're way braver than they are."

Arthur looked across the schoolyard at the gaggle of kids, and then back at her. His face split into a grin that looked like he'd just found his purpose in life.

At home, Jay was punished by not being allowed to watch television, which didn't bother her much, as she just read more books. But she endured two days of lectures from both parents about her behavior, until they found that bickering with each other was more to their taste.

Fed up with their arguing, she went outside after supper one night and looked in all directions, seeing nothing but flat, open fields of corn. It made her feel like Dorothy in Kansas. That made her remember the scarecrow, and she looked for it off in the distance.

Jay got out her bike from the garage, and pedaled along the country road to where she could see the scarecrow sticking up from the high green stalks of corn. She stepped off the road, set down her bike, and hiked through the tall plants. It was no trouble to move between the even rows, but she had to be careful to keep a straight line, because the corn was taller than she was, and it would be easy to get lost. The ground smelled dark and wild from rain the day before. Still, she got covered with pollen that stuck to her as she brushed the stalks.

Jay felt like she had biked a long way, but she didn't know where the scarecrow was. She jumped up as high as she could, trying to peek over the corn, and caught a glimpse of his hat. She walked in that direction, and soon saw the scarecrow on a slight bump in the field. She moved up the little hillock and stood next to the post, looking up.

From a ways off, the scarecrow looked like the

one from the *Wizard of Oz*, with old clothes and straw sticking out of the cuffs and neck. But when she peered at the face under the crumpled black hat, it was leathery brown and distorted, like a shriveled apple. It was totally creepy, because it did look kind of like a smushed face. She reached up to touch the pants, and jumped back. That was not soft stuffing inside, but instead felt like a very solid leg. There was a chemical smell that made her ill.

Ice water seemed to run down Jay's back as she realized this was a real dead body. She whirled around with a wild gaze, looked to the road, and began to run.

"Dad! Mom!" Jay exploded into the room.

"Pipe down." Her father's command stopped her. "*Wheel of Fortune*'s on. And don't slam the door like that. It's what makes it stick."

"But Dad! There's a *dead body*!"

Her father looked away from the television. "What?"

"A dead body."

"Where?"

"The scarecrow out in the field. It's not a scarecrow. It's real."

Her father looked at her. Her mother tittered. "She saw the scarecrow and asked me if it was Jesus."

"What?"

"You know, Jesus. Arms out, on the cross?"

Her father laughed. "Okay, very funny. Now let me watch my show."

"But Dad, it's a real dead body."

"Ah. You're lucky; it's a commercial. Now what's all this nonsense?"

"I rode my bike out to see it, but it's not just a dummy. It was a person hanging out there."

Her father chuckled. "Little early for a Halloween prank, and a little late for April Fool's Day." He turned to her mother. "What do you know about this?"

Her mother raised a hand. "I think someone's just a little bored since we stopped her television privileges. Okay; you win, Jay. You can watch TV again."

"It's not a prank!" Jay shouted, stomping her foot. They both stared at her. "It's a *real* dead body. Come with me and see, if you don't believe me."

Her father sighed. "Show's back on," he said, distracted. "We'll go in the morning."

"We should go *now*," Jay insisted.

"Why? If it's a dead body, it's not going anywhere, is it?"

Jay almost cried with frustration, but her father was yelling at the TV. "You need an 'A'! Ask for an 'A'!

"I think it's an 'E'," said her mother.

Jay could have smashed the television. She thought of calling the police, but knew with a sinking feeling that they wouldn't believe her either.

The next morning, Jay awoke and raced down the stairs. "Where's Dad?"

"He's not up yet," her mother said.

"But we have to go see."

"Oh, are you still playing that game?"

"Mom, it's not a game. I saw a dead body."

"Why don't you get ready for school?"

"Dad said we were going to see it."

Her mother slammed down a plate. "You're just like him. Nag until you get what you want. God, I'm so tired of it."

Jay bit her lip and left the kitchen. Why wouldn't they listen? Did they think she was a liar?

With no recourse, she got ready for school. Her father finally got up, shuffling to the kitchen.

"Hey, pumpkin," he said.

"Dad, you said we'd go out and check it, so you could see."

"Check what?"

"The dead body."

Her father frowned. "Don't you have school?"

"But you promised!"

"You might as well," her mother said. "Or we'll never hear the end of it."

"Fine," her father said. "Let me have some coffee and get dressed. I suppose I'll have to take you all the way to school afterward."

"Thanks, Dad." Jay almost hugged him.

After what seemed like a hundred years, her father was finally ready. They got in the car and drove out along the road, and parked on the dirt shoulder. Jay led her father through the corn, brushing aside the tall stalks which stood like sentinels. Her father kept shaking his head, as if anticipating a joke.

Jay followed her path from the day before, trailing the bent spears of plants. She reached the hillock and triumphantly looked up. Up came her father, huffing like an inefficient engine, and Jay could see he was uncomfortable and irritated, sweat already appearing on his brow and shirt.

But something was wrong. The face of the scarecrow was now just a burlap sack with white chalk marks for the crude set of eyes and mouth. The hat and other clothes were the same, though. She felt the leg, and it gave, straw falling out the bottom.

"So let's see this body," her father said. His hands were on his knees as he gasped for breath.

"It's . . . changed. This isn't it."

"What do you mean?"

"Dad, this isn't the scarecrow from yesterday. This is all straw."

"Well, that's what scarecrows are."

"You don't understand. This isn't what I saw yesterday. Someone took down the body and put this up instead."

"That's about what I thought," said her father. His shoulders were set, and his jaw was clenched. "But I wanted to give you the benefit of the doubt. Let's go to school now."

"But . . ." Jay wanted to fight, to convince him that someone had swapped the bodies, but nothing she could say would matter. She wouldn't change his mind. "I'm sorry, Dad."

"Yeah, me too."

At school, she got a chance to tell Arthur about the body at lunchtime.

"Whoa," he said. "That's pretty spooky."

"But my dad doesn't believe me."

"*I* believe you."

"Thanks," she said, and meant it. "Who would do that, put up a body?"

"Well, that's Old Man Perkins' land. He's a creepy old guy, that's for sure. Got a mean dog, too—barks at everyone."

"I can't figure how it was a body one day and then just a scarecrow the next."

Arthur furrowed his brow. "They say he watches people with his binoculars all the time, you know. Maybe he saw you out there, and knew you'd tell, so he switched it overnight."

Jay nodded. "Arthur, you're a genius!"

He beamed.

"Should we tell the police?"

Arthur gave her a pitying look. "Grown-ups *never* believe us. They'll just call you a liar."

"You're right," she admitted. "So, how do we catch him?"

"Catch him? Holy cow."

"Well, if that was a real body, he's a bad guy, right?"

"You really are a superhero."

She lightly punched his arm. "Does that make you my sidekick?"

"Guess it does."

"Then tell me how we're going to turn him in."

"It's like we're the Hardy Boys," Arthur said, a light in his eyes.

"Nancy Drew," Jay said. They laughed. Jay wrinkled her brow. "I wonder how long that body was out there, and nobody saw."

Arthur shrugged. "Out here in farm country,

folks just don't go out into other people's fields. And they see what they expect to see: just some old scarecrow like in every other field. I probably passed that field a hundred times and never noticed."

"I wonder who it was. Anybody go missing around here?"

Arthur looked at her. "You mean, like the people that were in your house?"

"What?"

"The place you live in now. The owners disappeared years ago. I was just a little kid, but I've heard people mention it from time to time."

"I thought my parents said they moved away after their son died."

"He was murdered," Arthur said solemnly.

Jay was shaken. "My parents didn't say anything about that."

"They probably didn't want to scare you."

"So what happened?"

"They found him by the side of the road, about ten miles from here. He'd been drinking beer, and somebody cut his throat. My brother told me all this."

Jay swallowed. This was serious stuff. "They catch who did it?"

"Yeah, some guy from the next town over had just gotten out of jail. He said he didn't do it, but they put him right back in. They were trying to execute him and everything. Then those people that had your house just disappeared. Nobody ever heard from them again."

"Holy cow," said Jay. She bit her lip. Since she was using his phrase, she wondered if they were on the same wavelength. "Are you thinking what I'm thinking?"

Arthur's eyes grew wide. He gulped. "You mean maybe they got the wrong guy, and the real killer is still out there?"

"Yeah."

Despite the stifling heat that continued all through September, Jay and Arthur rode out together every few days to check the scarecrow, but it remained just a straw-stuffed dummy on a pole. If it hadn't been for Arthur, Jay might have eventually believed she'd imagined it.

Jay's problems at school grew worse, despite that the socking she had given Roger had convinced the other kids to give her a wide berth, unless they were in a group. She'd found that by always responding with the correct answers to the questions the teachers asked made the other kids call her a smarty-pants-know-it-all. So she stopped raising her hand. The school librarian eyed her suspiciously when she tried to check out a stack of books. She was told the books were too advanced for her age, though she'd been reading much harder books for a long time. So she had to sneak some out and back in again, always afraid she'd get caught.

At home, things were even worse. Her parents fought all the time, and the house did not get fixed. Every time she went by the pictures of the former owners, she felt a shiver. She started having nightmares.

October crept in, and with it, the corn harvest. Huge machines chugged along the roads, as did trucks full of the reaping, and everywhere was the kicked-up dust that saturated the air and left a coating on anything exposed to the outdoors. People at school spoke in earnest tones about which fields had been harvested, and yields per acre, and Jay was bored to death. Her parents had gone from fighting to barely speaking, and she felt even more like she lived in a house of ghosts.

The only thing she was looking forward to was Halloween. It was a chance to dress in costume and become the character she wanted to be, rather than who she was, a girl being punished for something she didn't know she'd done.

"You're going to the Haunted Hayride, aren't you?" Arthur asked during lunch one day.

"What's that?" Jay took another bite of her peanut butter and jelly sandwich.

"We don't trick-or-treat around here; the houses are too far apart. But there's a farmer with a wagon who takes kids around the fields in the dark. We wear our costumes and some of the other parents and older kids dress up and make noises and jump at us, and some throw candy. It's pretty scary, but a lot of fun. Then there's bobbing for apples and a couple of games and stuff."

"That does sound like fun."

"There's just one problem. The farmer is old Mr. Perkins." Arthur sipped his milk and watched her face.

Jay's eyes went wide. "Holy cow."

"Yeah, he's the only farmer with a big, old-style wagon and horses, and he does it every year. People help set up the games inside his barn."

Jay tried to swallow. "Well, I guess this is our chance to look around for clues."

Arthur sighed. "I was kind of afraid you'd say that."

Jay started thinking. "What costume are you going to wear?"

"A cowboy."

"I'm going as a pirate," said Jay. "No one tells pirates what to do. They roam the seas, seeking adventure. You won't find them stuck in the middle of a cornfield."

She thought some more. "Make sure to wear dark colors, so we'll blend in with the night. We'll slip away at some point and look around. What about that dog you said he had?"

Arthur furrowed his brow. "I can take care of that."

The next day, Arthur gave her a small canister.

"What's this?"

"Pepper spray. Careful. Aim it, and with one squeeze of that right there, no animal will get near you. Makes their eyes water, and their throat close all up."

"Where'd you get it?"

"My brother's got a trunk with all kinds of cool stuff in it, knives and ninja stars and things. He says he'll never get his throat cut. I can pick the lock, but he'd kill me if he knew I touched his stuff. It'll keep you safe, but just make sure to give it back after."

Jay began piecing her costume together. A dark-colored handkerchief to cover her hair. An eye patch, with a loop of string to go around her head. A big, loose shirt of her father's he no longer wore. Boots, to which she added a cuff of fabric around the top of each, like she'd seen in a picture. Some of her mother's makeup, to paint a scar on her cheek. Some glitzy costume jewelry: a ring, a clip-on earring, some bracelets, and a necklace.

And of course she needed a weapon. No way her parents were going to let her carry a real blade, so she'd bought a cheap plastic sword from the dime store in town. But it had broken apart the first time she played with it, the plastic blade nothing but a hollow core that split from the handle. She studied it, and figured out how to make a real weapon.

From the torn-up pieces around the house, she selected a shard of hard material that her father had said was Formica. She inserted this into the hollow handle of the store sword, and covered it with the gray plastic blade. She ran a loop of masking tape around the outside to hold it in place. So it still looked like the cheapo sword, but now it had a real enough blade inside, like a secret weapon.

All day long Jay was fidgety and excited. She barely ate her dinner. She dressed in her costume with great care, putting a fearsome-looking scar on her cheek. She checked herself in the mirror. *Pretty cool,* she thought. The little canister of pepper spray was snug within a pocket. She still felt afraid, but she had weapons, like a real pirate.

Arthur's mother had agreed to give her a ride, and came to pick her up. Arthur was in the back seat, wearing a dark outfit, with a black cowboy hat and gun belt. He said he was Paladin, the TV cowboy hero.

At the farm, they walked past the parked cars. The farmer's house was on their left, and from the top of the porch, a pair of jack-o'-lanterns gaped down at them. A chained dog next to the porch barked incessantly. In the illumination from the big yard lights, they saw other kids from their school grouped in small knots of ghosts, caped heroes, witches, and princesses. From the barn came a recording of spooky Halloween sound effects: creaking doors, maniacal laughter, shrieks and howls.

Excited shouts erupted from the crowd of kids. "There it is. There's the wagon!"

The outside of the wagon was covered in cardboard bats and goblins and all manner of scary creatures. In the back were bales of straw to sit on, with fake spider webs in the corners.

Jay's flesh crawled when she caught sight of the wagon driver. Old Mr. Perkins was dressed as a scarecrow.

"Oh my god," she moaned. "It's for real."

Her legs seemed to turn to rubber, and she didn't know if she could stand. She couldn't get into that wagon; she just couldn't.

"Everybody's getting on. They don't know," said

Arthur. "But we know. What are we going to do?" He sounded like he wanted to cry.

Jay squeezed his hand. "We're going to get on the wagon. We have to. Maybe he doesn't suspect us yet. But even if he does, there's people all around. He won't try anything."

"I don't think I can do it."

She looked at him. "Would Paladin do it?"

Arthur licked his lips. "Yeah."

"And you're Paladin, right?"

"Right." His voice was a quaver.

"So let's get on. We'll sit in the back."

The wagon took off with a lurch and the kids squealed. The wheels crunched their way over the dry cornstalks, while ghostly moans and growling came from the darkness all around. Kids hugged one another as costumed monsters leapt out of the dark, pounding the sides of the wagon and grabbing at the passengers, eliciting screams of happy terror. Candy showered upon the passengers, and each time they yelled in surprise. They seemed happy to see what mock horror would happen next. All except Arthur, who remained almost petrified with fright, and Jay, who stared at the back of the driver in the scarecrow outfit as she clutched her makeshift sword.

The jolting wagon made its circuit in the dark, finally coming back around to the yard by the house. Jay was the first one off, pulling Arthur after her. They retreated to a safe distance as several volunteers got the last kids from the wagon. The scarecrow clucked to his horses and rode off.

"Everyone's going to the barn," said Jay. "Now's our chance."

"I'm scared."

"Me too. That's why I need you here."

"What if he comes back?"

"We'll be quick. Come on."

No one was looking at them while they darted across the yard, skirting the shadows. Jay looked up at the jack-o'-lanterns glowing from atop the porch railings, high up off the ground.

A large shape rushed at her, and she glimpsed teeth in a savage mouth. She recoiled as the dog barked furiously at her. It had reached the end of its chain, for which she was extremely grateful, since she suspected the animal would have torn her to pieces.

"Look at those," she whispered to Arthur, pointing up. "Do they look like pumpkins to you?"

"I can't tell," he said. "Let's go to the barn."

"In a minute. I want to get a closer look. Hold my sword."

She scrambled onto the porch railing and stretched up. The jack-o'-lanterns were still out of reach. She looked at the closer one and thought she could see a dark patch, like a birthmark, over one eyehole. Her stomach lurched, and she almost fell. She carefully climbed down.

"Okay, let's go now." They quickly made their way to the barn.

"What did you see?"

"Nothing." If she told him they might be hollowed-out human heads, not pumpkins, he would freeze in panic. People saw what they expected to see, so no one would imagine someone they knew would put up a couple of real human heads on their porch. From the ground, they looked pretty much like typical Halloween decorations.

She knew the farmer was the killer. That *had* been a real body hung out in the field. He must have seen her out there, taken the body down that night, and put up the regular scarecrow. And now he put these heads up right in front of everyone. He liked having his victims out where people would see them, but nobody would recognize what they were.

She'd tell Arthur later, after they had gone from here. He was scared enough already. They spent the next two hours shivering in fear on the edges of the crowd. She didn't fully breathe until the car had pulled away from the farm.

When she got home, she put her sword on the table by the front door and stripped off her patch, handkerchief, and jewelry. She went straight to her room and got ready for bed. But she took the small canister with her.

Jay lay awake for hours, her mind and heart racing. With no other recourse, she would have to tell her parents, but would they actually listen, or still think she was playing a joke? She'd make them listen. She'd have to make a plan with Arthur, figure out what to say.

But when Arthur wasn't in school the next day, Jay panicked. Had Perkins gone after Arthur? Jay was in a torment, trying to decide whether or not to go to her teacher and tell her everything. A dozen times she was on the verge of letting it all out. But each time, she remembered that the grown-ups would assume she was telling a tale. She needed some kind of proof. Maybe she could get one of those heads from Perkins' porch.

Somehow she made it through until school ended. The bus ride home seemed to stretch into endless hours.

"Mom? Dad?" Jay could hear the television when she got home, which was usual. But there was no response. She called again, louder. She walked into the kitchen and looked around. She had to call Arthur, but she glanced at the kitchen table, and her blood turned icy. There were two jack-o'-lanterns sitting there. And though horribly distorted, they looked familiar.

Oh no.

The pantry door flew open, and Jay was shocked to see Perkins come out, dressed once more like a scarecrow.

"Like my little present?" he cackled with a wild sound. "I made them special, just for you."

Jay could make no sound, only backed away. Her hand was in her pocket.

"I was coming for you all anyway," the man went on. "First you, then your little friend. I do so love this time of year. Anything can happen. Unhappy people who don't belong can just disappear forever. Or reappear as my souvenirs." He waved a hand at the display on the table. "We can get the family back together. I heard your name was Jacqueline. I think you will make a very fine Jackie Lantern."

He lunged toward her, and Jay brought out the little canister. She shot a jet of pepper spray into his face, and he fell back, screaming in pain and surprise. Eluding his flailing arms, she scooted out of the kitchen and down the hall toward the front door. She was almost there when she heard a growl. She turned in time to see a dark form attacking from the side. She sprayed another jet from the canister. The dog struck her, knocking her down, but whined in pain and staggered off. She had dropped the cylinder when she was struck, and struggled to get to her feet. She had to get away from the madman, get out the door, and run.

Here he came, screaming horribly, just as she grasped the doorknob and pulled. But the door that always stuck didn't open. Desperate, she looked at the little table that held the remnants of her Halloween costume. She grabbed for the sword and yanked the plastic cover off. She turned, screaming, and drove the pointed end into the madman as he closed in on her. The force of his attack knocked her backwards against the door.

He was standing still, looking at the absurd plastic sword hilt sticking out of his chest. He staggered a step or two, and fell to his knees. His mouth opened, but no sound came out. He fell over onto his side, and Jay was able to breathe again.

Still shaky, she went to the telephone. Now they'd believe her, finally . . . long after it was too late.

And she was determined, more than ever, that they would call her by whatever name she chose.

OLD MAN'S WINTER

Stacey Longo

Life was not fair, the old man knew. He'd known this ever since he was a child, when his world had been perfect and his parents had doted on him daily . . . until his little sister came along. Then, all of a sudden, he'd had to share his cookies, his rocking horse, and worst of all, his parents' time.

The old man did not take unfairness well. He felt balance should be restored as swiftly as possible. Which is why, at the tender age of six, he'd lured his sister out to the rocks behind their house to kill her.

Patsy, three years his junior, worshiped him even at that young age, and toddled after him everywhere he went on her red, chubby legs. The old man didn't care for this behavior one bit. Patsy following him meant that every picture book he looked at, every Play-Doh can he opened, became communal property. If he pinched his sister when she reached for a handful of colored dough, she'd wail for their mother until he had to let her play with him just to shut her up. Not fair at all.

Eyeing the sharp rocks in their backyard one morning over chocolate chip pancakes, the old man formed a plan. Not a perfectly thought-out plan, of course—he was only six, after all—but more of an idea of how he could be rid of the Patsy problem.

"Hey Patsy," he said through a mouthful of pancake, "wanna play hide and seek after breakfast?"

She nodded and clapped her hands, probably excited that her brother was offering to play with her. He told his mother they were going out back for a while, and she just nodded and waved them off, distracted by the dirty breakfast dishes she was soaping up. The old man led his sister past the spring daffodils to the craggy rocks, and she teetered for a moment at the top of one, almost doing his job for him. But she veered away from the edge of the sharp drop, giggling as she waddled back to his side. He took his sister firmly by the hand, led her back to the edge, and pushed.

His sister disappeared over the side without a word. The old man peered down to see the girl sitting in the dust six feet below.

"Patsy?" he called out. She looked up at him, tears starting to form, stunned but seemingly unhurt. This would not do. He grabbed a stone, scrambled down the rock to where she sat, and smashed the chunk of bedrock into his little sister's head until her skull caved in. And that had been that.

He'd blamed her demise on an accidental fall, and his parents had believed him—the truth would have been inconceivable to them—and once again, the old man's universe had fallen back in order, with his mother and father hugging him, their only remaining child, even tighter.

The old man's father had been a chemist at Pfizer, working at the plant in Groton for forty-four years until he dropped dead of a heart attack in the laboratory, shattering the Petri dish he was holding. He had been instrumental in developing the rabies vaccine, and when he'd died, he'd left his wife a healthy estate. The old man's mother was devastated by the loss. Six months after her husband's death, she suffered a stroke, and retreated to her bed, waiting for death to reunite her with her beloved chemist.

But the old man had plans, and taking care of his mother while she withered away in her shadowed room was not among them. He waited patiently until he hit eighteen years of age; he was now a high school graduate, young, ambitious . . . and just the right age to be able to inherit. The old man crept into his mother's room one chilly spring evening, listening to her steady breathing, punctured occasionally by a despondent sigh. He pushed a pillow over her face, bracing himself for a struggle, but none came. His mother died quietly, perhaps grateful for the release. The old man never really stopped to dwell on his mother's consent to her own death. He simply collected his inheritance, and continued on his life's path.

The old man got into fights and screaming matches around town when he felt slighted, which was often. When a black Thunderbird with oversized tires double-parked outside the local bar, effectively blocking in the old man's modest Falcon van, the old man had been furious. He took a baseball bat to the gaudy sports car and methodically smashed in all the windows. He never apologized for his actions, not even in court. He couldn't understand why the judge didn't see the problem: the overstuffed hyena in the Thunderbird had *double parked* and *blocked him in*. Case closed. Which it was, to the tune of a $200 fine.

The old man knew he was smarter than most, richer than most, and just out-and-out clever, and could not comprehend why his neighbors didn't respect and admire him. If the old man told you your dog needed to be on a leash, well, that was the truth of it, plain and simple. When the neighbor two doors down refused to keep his Rottweiler tied up, the old man poisoned it. He simply couldn't tolerate ignorance.

Because his temper was so well known on the streets of Groton, the old man moved to a more rural area of the state, buying himself a hundred acres to guarantee himself privacy from nosy neighbors. He started going to the local Methodist church's summer picnics to find a hardy, simple girl that might swoon when he courted her. Mary fit the bill. She was meek, plain, and god-fearing, and the old man liked that. If she feared and revered her god so much, well, it bode well that she might feel the same way about him. He proposed to her one steamy August night, so hot that even the mosquitoes couldn't muster up the energy to bite. Mary—young, innocent, and perhaps not very bright—said yes.

They married, and he never set foot in church again, much to Mary's chagrin. The first time she nagged at him to come back to the flock, he punched her hard enough to knock out a molar. She never asked again.

Mary bore him two sons, two years apart. The first was named Junior, after him; the younger boy was Henry. Junior was brilliant and bold with dark, hard features like the old man. Henry was quiet and watchful and as blond and soft as his mother. The old man focused all of his attention on his elder son, teaching him how to stand up for himself in the most concrete of terms. A note soon came home from school in Junior's book bag with threats from the teachers to not let Junior back the next day, due to the brutal sucker punches he'd been doling out at recess. This would not do, and the old man now faced the problem of Junior's behavioral issues. He beat the problem out of his son with a heavy belt.

As Junior got older, his brother became his favorite target, and Henry took to hiding in the dark corners of the barn out back to avoid his brother's haymakers. The old man encouraged his sons to work out their problems with their fists; it would toughen them up as men. Henry often sported a black eye or a makeshift sling on his arm, until right before his sophomore year of high school. That summer, he hit a growth spurt that left him four inches taller and sixty pounds heavier than his brother. Henry waited for the right moment, to meet Junior blow for blow and fight back. He didn't have to wait long—Junior attacked him one morning for using up the rest of the milk in his morning cereal—but Henry found he *couldn't* fight back. Much as he hated being his brother's punching bag, he realized he had no choice. The old man might well kill him for hitting his brother, and kill Junior for losing a fight. Henry sighed and let his brother's fists rain down upon him once again. Mary had to rush Henry to the hospital with a broken jaw.

The old man was furious just the same. He'd decided to run for town council that fall, and he couldn't have his idiot sons messing up his chances with gossip-inspiring breaks and bruises. He boxed Junior's midsection until the boy fell to the ground, retching; then he grabbed his younger son by the back of his neck and whipped him around to teach him a lesson about keeping up appearances. To his surprise, the son's fist met the father's nose in such an explosion of pain that the old man was on his knees before he knew what hit him.

Angrily he cancelled his plans to shake hands and kiss babies at the town's spaghetti supper planned for that evening. He couldn't go with a swollen face and broken nose; this was exactly the kind of behavior and bruising he'd been trying to teach his boys wouldn't be tolerated. There was no room in the old man's life for troublemakers. Even that infernal Bible that Mary kept on the living room table said to honor thy father. After he had his nose set, the old man kicked Henry out of the house, disowning him. He forbade Mary from seeing her baby boy, the one that was so like her.

Mary disobeyed his order only once, walking four miles down the road to meet Henry at Bolton Lake and slip him a few dollars she'd stolen from her husband's wallet. The old man heard her that morning, sifting through his jacket pockets, and as soon as she'd gently closed the front door behind her, he'd gotten up and followed her. He'd traded in the Falcon for a Marquis a year earlier, a much quieter car that allowed him to hang back unnoticed as he stalked her. He turned three shades of purple when he saw who she was meeting. Mary had disobeyed him, and she would have to pay.

That night over dinner, a passable meat loaf that Mary knew was his favorite, he asked her what she'd done that day. She spoke of weeding the front flower bed and hemming a pair of his socks. The old man reached over and neatly snapped her pinky finger, breaking it. He asked again, but she didn't seem to want to answer between her shrieks of pain. The old man finished breaking all of the fingers on her right hand, then tucked in to his meatloaf. He did not tolerate thieves.

After dinner, he found Mary sitting in the bathroom, crying softly.

"I'm sorry," she whimpered. "It's just—he's our

son."

"No, he's not. Not anymore. If I catch you doing that again—"

"You'll kill me?" she asked, looking down at her mangled hand.

"Hell, no. I'll kill *him*. And you'll have to live with the knowledge that you were the one responsible for his death, by making me do it."

The old man was fairly sure he'd cured her of her disobedient ways, but for good measure, he waited until she was kneeling out in the garden among the wilting vines one crisp autumn morning, and then crept up behind her. She flinched when she heard his steps rustling in the leaves, but it was too late. He slammed the small of her back with a four by four. Mary was never able to stand completely upright again, which was, of course, what she deserved for crossing the old man. He was pretty sure her precious Bible said to honor thy husband, too.

When he'd moved to town years ago, the old man had invested in an abandoned quarry. He'd slowly leveled out the land and had started construction on a cheap housing development. Now that Mary stooped all the time, looking more and more like an old woman, the old man wasn't really interested in sleeping with her. He took up with the girl that kept his books for the development. She had hair red as flame and a great set of gams; the old man would have killed Mary if she'd ever dared to dress in skirts that ended right at the knee, but Red was different. A mistress could get away with things that a wife could not, and Red was a real firecracker. Until he found her one evening crying in the dark shack she used as an office at the construction site. Red was pregnant; the old man would have to divorce Mary and wed her, or she would be ruined—ruined!—in their small town. The old man took her for a walk around the site, his arm over her shoulders, consoling her. Then he let his rough hands circle her throat, strangling her without a sound. He laid her body out like a starfish in the bottom of a foundation that was set to be poured in the morning. The old man was not afraid of a little hard work, and he poured the foundation by himself that night, smoothing out the cement until it was perfectly even, just as dawn broke. When Red's father came by the site a few days later, the old man immediately began yelling at him.

"Tell your irresponsible daughter that if she can't show up for work, I'll find someone who will!" he roared. He ranted and bellowed until the worried father was forced to give up and leave, never able to ask if anyone there had seen his little girl.

Junior had no interest in his father's business, and left home after high school to join the army. He was killed in Vietnam eight months later, and for a moment, reading the telegram, the old man felt something akin to sadness. He quickly chalked it up to heartburn. The day of Junior's funeral, the old man had a council meeting, and needed to get his hair trimmed and groomed beforehand. After all, he considered himself a pillar of society, and needed to look the part. He acquiesced, however, to let Mary go. After all, it might look bad if neither parent went to their son's service.

Junior's grave lay unmarked for years. The old man was outraged at how much even the smallest gravestones cost. He'd be damned if he were going to spend that kind of money just to mark where his idiot son's rotting corpse was buried. *Not my problem,* he figured, and eventually, the local veterans' services paid for a steel plate marker to honor their town's fallen son.

It was just the old man and Mary after that. Mary hobbled off to church three days a week, praying for salvation, or at the very least, escape. The good Lord was merciful, giving Mary cancer in her female parts. She refused to go to the doctor for surgery or radiation, which was fine with the old man. He thought all doctors were crooks, and although Mary was growing thinner and grayer every day, she had a quality about her the old man didn't ever remember her possessing. It took him some time to recognize it: something like . . . satisfaction.

Mary died in November, and the old man ran an obituary in the paper, listing himself as her only living survivor. The paper charged five cents a word, so he kept it brief, just three sentences. He settled into his retirement, letting Mary's garden go to seed. He lost his seat on the town council to a returning vet, and that was okay, because his bones were starting to ache every time the weather changed. His hair turned white as snow, and even the Jehovah's Witnesses stopped visiting his house after he threatened them with a shotgun. He had his prescriptions for the arthritis in his knees delivered to his home along with his groceries, and he spent his days in front of the television, sipping a Pabst Blue Ribbon and watching the fights every Friday night.

He was surprised the day Henry broke into his house and stood in the living room, blocking the old man's view of the Zenith. The old man would've been perfectly fine with never seeing his younger son again, but here he was. Henry looked good for sixty, though his hair was thinning, and his face was creased with the same lines that had been permanently furrowed in Mary's forehead.

"Hello, Pop," Henry said lightly.

"Not your father," the old man mumbled, perturbed. The highlights from the Holyfield fight were supposed to re-run in just a few minutes.

"Won't take but a moment of your time. The house," Henry paused, looking around. "Jeez, the house is a pigsty. And it's freezing in here. Is the furnace on?"

"Broken. Repairs cost money. Don't have a lot of money," the old man huffed, and Henry laughed.

"You sly old liar. You've got more money than Rockefeller. You're just too stingy to spend a dime of it." Henry grinned, a toothy, pained smile, and the old man scowled.

"Whattaya want, you little bastard? I'm busy."

"Sure you are, sure you are. I can see that. I just wanted to stop by and let you know how I've been, Pop. Got married, which I guess you would have known if you'd gone to Junior's funeral, seeing as Gail came with me. Anyway, no matter. She left me," he sighed, waving his weathered palms as if to push this news about his failed marriage aside. "She said I had issues. I suppose I do. Always have. I like to think I got them from you." Henry stopped a moment to cough.

The old man watched him from hooded, rheumy eyes. Then he let a cruel smile crawl across his lips. "Always knew you'd be a failure, even at marriage. Your mother was with me 'til the day she died," the old man boasted.

"Yup. I know," Henry said, nodding. "We kept in touch, you know, even after you broke her fingers, you cruel bastard. I went to church every Sunday just to see her. What a rotten life she had with you. You bullied the will to live right out of her. Hope you're happy."

The old man was frowning, furious. How dare she—his wife!—behind his back, after he'd *ordered* her—he struggled to stand, ready to take out his anger on his disgraceful spawn. Henry pushed him back down on the couch easily.

"She's dead; you can't punish her any more. And what do you think you can do to me? See, here's the thing, Pop. I've spent a lot of years struggling, wishing for one thing, just one little thing, my whole life. But here you are, still living and breathing, right as rain." Henry shook his head. "Guess it's true what they say: evil never dies."

The old man clenched his fists. He refused to let this snotnosed punk talk to him so disrespectfully. The old man was a pillar in the community, what with all he'd done, filling in the quarry and building new homes. Serving on town boards. Why, every year, he'd even donated twenty dollars to the Auxiliary Club for their fundraiser. He wasn't about to let Henry *disrespect* him—

"Relax, Pop. I'm here to tell you something you'll probably enjoy," he continued, scratching his chin. "I've been diagnosed with terminal cancer. It's too far along and all over my pancreas and my liver. Got only a few months to live," Henry said, and the old man couldn't help himself. He laughed.

"Yeah, I thought that would cheer you up, you wretched bully. But here's the thing, Pop. I've got just one thing on my bucket list I want to get to before I die. That's why I'm here." Henry smiled, pulling out a gun that had been tucked in his back waistband. "Seeing you dead has been at the top of my to-do list for years."

The old man blinked. His boy was pointing a pistol right at his head, and for the briefest of moments, he was shocked. Then he broke out in a wide grin.

"Not so unlike me after all," the old man beamed, as his son pulled the trigger.

SCALPER

David Daniel

Vic Dempsey shuffled out of the Garden with thirteen thousand other hometown fans. The Bruins had lost to the Oilers, but the game had been a thriller, right down to the go-ahead goal with a minute on the clock. At one point both benches emptied, gloves and sticks dropped, punches flew.

When he reached the bottom of the tunnel ramp, Vic checked his watch. 9:35 P.M. There was time for a beer before his train left. He was still pumped from the action.

Crossing the concourse at North Station, en route to the Penalty Box bar, he heard a grunt, followed by a smacking sound. He peered into a shadowy alcove and saw two men going at each other with fists. With a nudge of interest, Vic glanced about for a cop; saw none. He edged nearer.

A knot of watchers had gathered. One of the fighters looked to be in his mid-30s, Vic's age, the other younger, with cornrows and a denim jacket. Neither was doing much damage with his wild, roundhouse punches, but both had flushed, angry faces, and the crowd was into it, egging them on.

Just then a whistle shrilled. Several Transit Authority cops loomed. Vic turned up the collar of his topcoat and walked quickly away.

As he reentered the concourse, a man leaning against a pillar nodded at him. Slender, with crisp dark hair and a green satin Celtics jacket, the man was dimly familiar. Vic realized he had seen him before, had talked to him, if you could call it that. On several occasions the guy had tried to sell him game tickets. A scalper.

But the man made no pitch now. Instead, he tossed his head toward where the T Cops were leading away the pair of brawlers. "Clowns. Can't enjoy a game without gettin' loaded and belting someone. But I guess that's why people watch hockey."

With the assorted touts, louts, and hustlers that sporting events drew, it was Vic's habit to move past, but he felt the barb in the man's words. "I watch hockey for the strategy and skill," he said.

The scalper grinned. "Right, and people read *Hustler* for the articles. When the NHL bans fighting, people might just as well go watch the Ice Capades."

That did it. Vic's anger flared. "I don't notice you lodging any complaints. No fans, no profit for guys like you, huh?"

The man lifted his palms in a gesture of peace. "Hey, I don't create the need. I just try to satisfy it."

"I don't have that need," Vic said. "I'm a fan. I've got season tickets." He started toward the bar, eager for that beer, but the scalper sauntered along with him.

"Okay, hockey's sporting enough, I'll grant you. For a *game*. But take that slugfest just now. Kinda got the juices flowing for a minute there, didn't it? Tell me—hypothetical like . . . would you pay to see some real action?"

Vic frowned. "Two drunks pounding each other? Forget it."

"Actually, I had something else in mind." The man glanced around cautiously and lowered his voice. "You like dogs?"

"Dogs. You mean greyhound racing?"

"Ever seen pit bulls go at it?"

Vic stopped walking, not out of any genuine interest, he told himself, just shock. Naturally he had heard about fights where people bet money on dogs to maim or even kill each other, but no one he knew ever claimed to have seen one. Watching Vic closely, the scalper said, "I can get you pit-side for half a bill."

Vic returned his gaze. The man's face was calm and alert, intelligent even, in a street-hard way. Most of the people who hawked tickets around here were young, in saggy jeans and hoodies. This guy looked forty, with direct, watchful eyes and a soft voice. After a moment, Vic let his breath out in a laugh. "I'll stick to the NHL. At least *that* action's legal."

There was no hard sell. With a wave, the man

drifted away. Vic went into the bar, thought about beer, and then ordered whiskey.

It wasn't following the next Bruins game, but the one after that, that Vic paid the man in the Celtics jacket fifty dollars, and three nights later he sat among a small, worked-up crowd of strangers in a smoky basement in Chelsea and watched a pair of vicious, badly bred mongrels go at each other with snapping jaws. Afterwards he rode home, sickened but strangely excited.

Vic Dempsey had lettered in football and hockey in high school. In college, he focused his energies on studying marketing and pursuing coeds. In both he had been successful, and at 34 he was an assistant VP for a mid-sized Boston firm, a contented husband and father living in a leafy suburb. But the hours, the meetings, the commuting, the household duties, drained away the energy of his youth until mostly it was a longing memory. Sometimes a zest came back to him when he sat in the Garden or at a Pats game, or when he drove his BMW fast on I-93; but more and more there was a sense that he was no longer in control of his life. Some old hunger was gone. He missed those days.

One night in late spring, as he read his newspaper on the train platform, Vic heard someone say, "Hockey season's almost over."

Vic hadn't seen the scalper since the dogfight more than a month ago. The Celts jacket had given way to a Red Sox windbreaker. Vic felt a stir of interest. With a glance to be sure he wasn't overheard, the man said, "Up for some action?"

Vic drew a careful breath. "That last little number was . . ."—he almost said *unsettling*—". . . interesting. But once was plenty."

"I'm with you. Too bloody. Actually, I got something different, more spontaneous. But it's got to be tonight."

Vic shook his head. "You'll have to find another fan."

The scalper nodded. "Yeah, maybe this action's a little too strong for you," he agreed. "I'll catch you when there's somethin' tamer going down." He started to leave.

"Wait." The word was out before Vic knew it. He stuffed his newspaper into his briefcase. "There's another train in a couple hours."

Making random conversation about the Bruins' hopes for next season, and the Sox's for this, the man led him across the parking lot. For a few long minutes they walked, angling toward the waterfront, farther away from the downtown lights. Vic asked where they were going, but the scalper was evasive, and Vic discovered he liked the way his curiosity and excitement kept growing. "I just hope it's not going to take a lot of time," he said.

"Naw, it'll be brief. But memorable." The scalper stopped walking and turned. "And worth every cent of the three hundred."

"What?"

"That's the admission price."

"Three hundred bucks for a so-called sporting event? You're nuts! The Super Bowl doesn't even—"

"Look, I don't twist nobody's arm. You say no, we split. I don't hassle you. But if you want to watch, it's three bills."

Vic squawked a little, but it was only token resistance. He paid.

Soon they came to a small park, somewhere beyond the North End. Gas lamps flared in the April dark. Over the tenements, a pale moon was rising. The scalper drew Vic into the shadows of a clump of forsythia, its flowers ghostly in the dark.

"Why are we here?" Vic wanted to know.

"Hang tight a minute. Be right back." And before Vic could protest, the man slipped away.

Three minutes crept by. Five. Vic began to believe he'd been scammed. The moon silhouetted the rooftops and chimneys of the neighborhood, including the spire of the church where someone had once hung lanterns for Paul Revere. From the corner of his eye, Vic saw movement on the far side of the park. Tensing, he peered through the bushes and spotted an old man slowly walking a small dog. The man shuffled to a bench, sat down, secured the leash to the back post, and took a small paper bag from his pocket. Twisting at the top of the bag, he tipped it to his lips. Nothing else happened. The old man sat quietly in the dark, drinking.

A swell of frustration swept Vic; then disappointment; finally, anger. There was no show, wasn't going to be one. He felt like a yokel who'd fallen for a three-card monte scam. As he turned away, a muffled crash of glass startled him. Then barking.

Back across the park another figure had

appeared, tall and slender, in dark clothing. He stood behind the bench with one hand clapped over the old man's face. The little dog was hopping frenziedly, firing volleys of weak noise. Vic's heart was hammering. He had an impulse to rush over . . . until he saw a glint of metal in the mugger's hand.

Shakily the old man surrendered his wallet and his watch. Pocketing them, the mugger slapped the old man, turned and ran.

When Vic got there, panting from his own dash across the park, the little dog had tangled its leash around the bench. The old man was trembling with fright but insisting he wasn't hurt. More people arrived; someone called 911. Others began arguing over descriptions of a man they'd seen fleeing. Vic left before the cops came and hurried to the train station with his heart still pounding.

It wasn't until he was aboard the train, gazing out at the moonlit night, that he understood: he had just paid to see a mugging.

Vic never asked the scalper's name. They met briefly several times after that, and money changed hands. One evening, for a five-hundred dollar "admission," Vic crouched behind packing crates in a moving company warehouse in Chinatown, along with a wide-eyed middle-aged couple, and watched while a man was tried before a tribunal of hoods and sentenced to having an arm broken. The middle-aged husband declined an opportunity to see justice meted out, but the wife and Vic followed the scalper to a window overlooking an alley. From the thick shadows below they heard a damp *snap* of bone, then shrieks of pain.

Vic took those sounds home with him, guardedly bringing them to memory every once in a while, never without a churn in his gut and a quickening of his pulse. For a long time after the kangaroo court session, he drove his car to and from work, avoiding the train, and limiting his spectating to TV sports.

When he resumed commuting by train, he occasionally saw the scalper lurking around North Station, hawking sports tickets, and Vic would hurry away. Sometimes they would make eye contact, but there was no pitch, and Vic wasn't sorry. Not really. But the date for ordering Bruins season tickets came and went. Vic kept himself busy at the office and at home.

Then, one November evening, he lingered at the station, letting one, and then a second commuter train depart without him.

"Cold night."

Vic knew the voice before he turned.

"You're not waitin' inside like everyone else," the scalper said.

"I don't mind this weather," Vic told him, keeping interest out of his voice.

"It's good weather for some things," the scalper agreed, his breath drifting off in wisps.

"Anything . . . special in mind?" Vic asked it casually.

The scalper measured him for a moment. "How'd you like to catch a chill?"

Vic frowned, not understanding.

"*The* chill," the man said, his eyes narrowing.

"The big chill. See someone get iced."

Vic's heart gave a staggering little leap. Iced. Chilled. Smoked. His mind scurried through a catalogue of synonyms (*wasted, waxed, snuffed*) pulling up short of the most familiar of them all. God! This was going too far. *Way* too far! And all at once Vic realized he was heartsick at what he had already paid this man to watch—and what he had lingered around tonight hoping to see. *I'm as sick as he is!* Vic thought.

"Tonight, Mr. Dempsey," the scalper said matter-of-factly, and Vic was startled to hear his name. He'd never given it. Their exchanges had always been in cash. "Gotta be tonight."

Vic's head was whirling, turbulent in the crosscurrents of what was happening. This was insanity. Was he really being offered a chance to watch a murder take place? Or had he misunderstood? Maybe he should call time out and get this straight—or phone the police, report this . . .

And then the words he had spoken on other occasions came from him in a clear, though distant, voice. "How much?"

"This one's a double dime."

"*What?*"

"You heard me."

Two thousand dollars! Pulling a handkerchief from his pants pocket, Vic wiped his mouth. "Hell, I don't carry half that much."

The scalper laughed. "Of course not. But there's a cash machine in the lobby. I've seen you use it. You must be good for a quick infusion, Mr. D. Successful man like you. That's a nice Beemer you drive to work when you ain't riding the rails."

"They don't let you take out more than a certain amount at a time. I think it's three hundred."

"There's lots of cash machines around. Probably a dozen we could get to in ten minutes." The man shrugged. "It's up to you."

A cold breath of wind swept along the platform and brought Vic back to reality. He nodded, feeling his confusion fade.

Getting the money was as easy as the scalper said. When Vic had handed over the bills, he and the man picked their way through the financial district, deserted, dark, and windy at this hour. They didn't speak. Despite the cold, Vic felt heat coming off him like a blast furnace. His mind was working at fever pitch too, and in the past few moments he believed he had found a direction at last.

He had lost control of his life and had been playing in traffic, trying to compensate for the routine in his days by tramping on a sleazy nighttime edge of urban degeneracy, paying for dubious kicks. He got it now. He'd been wrong to do it, but he wasn't a sicko. He was going to confess everything to his wife, and to the police, too.

But what he had to do first, he had to stop the scalper. Get him arrested; overpower him even, if it came to that. Vic had a couple inches and thirty pounds on the man. Just how he would do this wasn't clear yet, but he would think of something. For the first time in a long while, Vic was beginning to feel in control again.

As he sometimes did, the scalper began to talk sports. Bruins, the Pats, the Red Sox's chances of besting the Yankees. Vic tried to keep up his end, but it was tough: his thoughts wouldn't focus on sports. Grown men playing kids games seemed absurd all of a sudden.

Soon they came to a plywood fence surrounding a construction site. In the dark it resembled a palisade. The scalper quit talking and looked at his watch. Motioning for Vic to follow him, he slipped through a concealed gap in the fence. Inside, they found themselves on the rim of a deep excavation pit for a large, soon-to-be-built structure. Below, iron reinforcing rods jutted from new concrete like bare saplings. Signaling silence, the scalper led the way down a gravel path. At the bottom, he drew Vic behind a stack of I-beams.

"How you doin', Mr. D?" he whispered.

"All right," Vic managed, though he was winded from the descent.

"Good. This is gonna be something special."

"What do—?"

"Shh."

Just then, across the site, a figure appeared. Vic jumped. "Easy," the scalper said. "Security guard."

The man was short, heavyset, in a quilted jacket and a Cossack hat. He was patrolling the site on a path that would bring him near to where they were hiding. The scalper looked at his watch again.

"What's . . . what's going to happen?" Vic's words were a wisp.

"You'll see. And so will he." From inside his coat the scalper drew a snub-nosed revolver.

Good God! So that was it. The guard was the target. Vic's mind began to scramble. He was sure the bang of his heart was audible.

The guard strolled nearer, oblivious to the hidden would-be killer and paying spectator. A nightstick swung harmlessly from his belt. His shoes crunched on the rutted ground as he got closer.

The scalper raised the revolver—

"*Guard!*" Vic yelled. He lunged, grabbed the scalper's arm, and they toppled against the I-beams. Steel cracked against his ribs, but he didn't break his grip. "Guard!" he shouted again. "Over here!"

The night around him whirled, and the ground below seemed to stagger, like a top that has lost its spin. Vic wobbled and fell into darkness.

Gingerly, Vic probed the knot on his head. It felt like a squash ball. As he struggled to sit up, he peered through a fog and saw the scalper standing nearby, holding the gun. The security guard was nowhere to be seen.

"That was a lousy trick," the scalper said. "You tried to ruin it."

Vic shook his head, and it cleared slightly. "You're sick."

"Am I? For someone in marketing, Mr. D, you got little knowledge of reality. And even less imagination. You're judging me. But if it wasn't for people like you, willing to pay for their kicks, I wouldn't exist. Don't nobody make a dime sellin' things no one wants."

Vic's head was slowly defogging. "What happens now?" he asked uncertainly.

The scalper shrugged. "Here's your money back."

As Vic took it, there was a faint sound of footsteps above. He squinted and saw a man in a ball cap moving in between the plywood barriers at the top of the excavation. Vic's heart leapt with hope. Two other men crowded in beside the first, then a woman, and another, older man. Vic wasted no time. "*Help!*"

The word ricocheted around the unfinished foundation with a flat concrete echo. "Get the cops!" he shouted hoarsely. "He's got a *gun!*"

The people had to have heard; several looked at each other, but, incredibly, nobody moved to act. Then the security guard appeared among them. He spoke to them a moment, words that Vic couldn't hear, and then the guard moved with cautious haste down the slope to where Vic and the scalper waited.

"Everybody pay?" the scalper asked.

The guard handed over a fistful of bills. "They're ready."

In the icy wind Vic's head cleared fully. "Jesus," he whispered, "am I . . .?" The thought died. "*Help!*" he cried.

The scalper looked up at the ring of people, who stared down unmoved, wide-eyed, hungry for action. Then, nodding, he handed the gun to the security guard, who thumbed back the hammer and aimed.

NEVER ALONE

Ursula Wong

Raymond lingered on the bench at the foot of Rasa's bed, listening to the music of her sleeping. Her room was cloudy in the dark, but its contents were familiar: the music box, the lamp with the fringe, the rocking chair, books neatly lined up on shelves like toy soldiers, her robe draped over the bench.

There was a shuffle of sheets and Rasa sat up, her eyes wide open. Raymond dropped to the floor. After a moment, Rasa's even breathing returned. He peeked at the bed. Her eyes were closed, and the corners of her mouth were relaxed in sleep.

He crept out of the room and went downstairs to the front window. The moonlight cast the barn in a silvery glow, and he remembered how it used to be.

"Daddy, wait for me!" Raymond said as he scrambled up the ladder to the hayloft. The wagon had come in from the field and the horses were swishing their tails as they waited for the men to unload. Uncle Joe stood on the wagon, his shoulders moving like a see-saw, trapping hay within the tines of the pitchfork, and lifting it up through the door into the loft. Raymond's father, in faded overalls, tossed the hay to Uncle Eddie, who tossed it on to Uncle Alex, who threw it onto piles where it would stay until winter. Hay was constantly in the air, flowing from man to man in a wave traveling through the barn. The dry grass smelled like toast. Bits of chaff hung in the air like snow.

Raymond's body tensed in a coiled spring. When the next forkful of hay became airborne, he raced to get to Uncle Alex before the hay did.

"Raymond, cut that out," said his father.

"What?" asked Raymond.

"It's too dangerous to run up here."

Raymond shuffled back to his father, and tossed pretend hay with a pretend pitchfork. When the wagon was empty, they climbed down.

"Can I go into the fields with you, Daddy?"

"Why don't you stay home and play with your brother?"

"All he wants to do is read. Please, can I come?" Raymond pulled at his father's hand.

"We have a lot of work to do and can't have you underfoot."

They approached the kitchen window where

Raymond's mother was handing out glasses of lemonade. Raymond tried to drink his in one breath like his father, who tossed his head back and gulped while a thin stream of liquid trickled down his neck. On the first swallow, Raymond coughed and snorted lemonade out his nose. The men laughed and patted him on the back as they walked to the wagon for the trip back to the field.

Raymond followed them until they disappeared through a gap in the stone wall. Then he climbed up the rocks and with his arms out to the side, stepped onto the imaginary tightrope strung high above the earth. He flailed his arms. The audience gasped. Raymond smiled down at upturned faces and voices shouting "Bravo!"

A bee buzzed past his ear and landed on a stone. Raymond crouched down and moved one hand to the barrel of the gun, and the other to the trigger. He had one shot. Only one of them would live.

"Kaboom!" Raymond lowered the rifle, stepped on a loose stone, and tumbled into a ditch.

He almost cried out to his mother, but she might think he was hurt and keep him inside for the rest of the day. Raymond got up, swatted the dirt off his breeches, and walked home.

He climbed the ladder to the loft. The men would be home soon. A breeze ruffled his hair. He stretched out his arms.

"Pum pum pum," he yelled. He was a pilot flying a biplane inside the barn. What daring! What skill! He careened past the opening, appearing and disappearing, each time stepping closer to the edge. He stepped where there was no floor, and he fell. He heard a thud when he landed, and then the world went away.

When he woke up, everything was different.

Raymond slid out of bed and stumbled down the hallway to his brother, who was sitting in a chair in his room, staring out the window. Clothes were all over the floor, as usual. Raymond touched his brother's shoulder. He didn't move.

"Wassa matter?" asked Raymond. His brother looked right at him, then turned back to the window. Raymond poked his brother in the arm. Raymond couldn't feel himself making the jabs. His brother just sat there. Raymond lifted his hands and could see right through them. This couldn't be! He ran downstairs, his feet banging on the floor with the intensity of rose petals drifting to the ground. He flew into the kitchen.

"Mommy, something's wrong with me," shouted Raymond. No one was there.

He found his parents and uncles sitting around the dining room table. Why was his mother crying? Why were the men inside during the day?

"Mommy, come look at me!"

She wiped her eyes.

"Here I am!" said Raymond, but no one looked up. He scrambled to the top of the table and kicked up his heels in a dizzying dance. No one said, "Get down from there, Raymond." No one even noticed him. Maybe they were playing a joke.

Raymond ran into the hallway and looked in the mirror. All he could see was a light gray haze. Something was wrong with *his* eyes, too.

Raymond was angry that they were ignoring him, especially since he was sick, so he stayed in his room all day. That would show them! But no one came to check on him. No one brought him supper. No one tucked him into bed. No one read him a story. After dark, he slunk through the house and listened to his mother say his name in her sleep. Then he leaned over his brother's bed and dared him to open his eyes. Nothing happened.

Raymond went back to his room and waited there for days. He began wandering through the house at night, pretending his family wanted to see him, but couldn't because of the dark.

Then one night, Raymond noticed boxes all over the house. Were they going somewhere? He didn't want to leave. He tried emptying the boxes and putting things back where they belonged, but everything he touched slipped through his fingers, except for some straw that fell to the floor in a little pile. The next day, strange men came into his room and took all his things while his mother watched from the doorway.

"Mommy, stop them!" Raymond pulled at her skirt. She dabbed her eyes with a handkerchief and then smoothed her skirt with her hands.

She followed the men downstairs, where Raymond's father and brother waited. A breeze blew in from the open door. Raymond wondered if it would toss him into the air like a feather and he would never come down. His family walked past him, out the door, and was gone. He wanted to follow them, but he was afraid of the wind.

He waited in the front hallway, willing a familiar face to appear. At daybreak, Raymond went to his room and curled up on the floor.

He didn't know whether a day, a week or a month had passed when he slumped into the kitchen and saw a strange lady sitting at the table. She had dark hair and brown eyes. The light flowed in a river through her hair. She was writing something on a sheet of paper.

He ran up to her. "Hi. I'm Raymond. Who are you?" The lady jerked her head up. Raymond's heart leapt. She looked toward the open window and went back to her writing.

"Hey." Raymond poked her shoulder with his finger.

The lady put her hand on her shoulder and rubbed.

Raymond bent around her and put his head on the table, right in front of her.

She dropped her pencil, strode to the window, and closed it. "I need to rest my eyes," she murmured.

How wonderful it would be if the lady took him by the hand and asked him his name, thought Raymond. She'd make him a cup of cocoa, tuck him into bed, and kiss his forehead. Maybe she'd even read him a story.

But she was acting as if he weren't even there.

Raymond stomped to the middle of the room and threw himself down on the floor. He kicked the wood with his fists and feet, and yelled, "Why can't you see me?" Raymond pounded the floor harder and harder.

The floor creaked.

Raymond stopped moving. He had made a noise! He rolled onto his back. She'd have to notice him now. He put his hands under his head, crossed his legs at the ankles, and smiled up at the ceiling.

The lady grabbed a pan from the stove, and held it up in the air. She walked right over to Raymond, who rolled away so she wouldn't step on him. The floor creaked again. The lady stared at Raymond. He smiled.

"Don't be an idiot, Rasa. It's just an old house," she said. She put the pan down and went back to the table and her writing. Every few minutes, she looked up and cocked her head to the side as if she was listening for something.

Raymond got up and looked over her shoulder at the paper. He read slowly, for he had to sound out some of the words.

Dear Peter:

I worry about you in the trenches and imagine how horrible it must be. The newspaper claims the war will be over soon and I wish for that with every waking moment. If thoughts could bring you home, you'd be with me now.

I finally moved our furniture into the new house. I decided on damask drapes for the living room. Even though they're expensive, I love them and know you will, too. The old house creaks and feels cold sometimes. The woman next door said that a little boy fell from the hayloft and died some time ago. I wonder whether it's his ghost I feel and hear, but it's silly for me to say such things when you are in danger. Forgive me for being a lonely woman who desperately misses her husband.

If the house frightens me, I'll find another. You won't mind, will you darling? As long as we're together, we are home, although I know you want a barn.

I pray for you in my dreams.
All my love, Rasa
P.S. Enjoy the socks. I knit them myself.

Raymond ran into the living room. It was full of unfamiliar furniture. He wondered if Rasa was writing about him. *He* had fallen from the hayloft. Was he really a ghost? He didn't want to be a ghost.

Raymond trudged up the stairs to his brother's room. The clothes were gone from the floor and a pink blanket covered the bed. If he made noises, Rasa might move away and he would be alone again. He rushed into his parent's room. Was he dead? He didn't feel dead. Instead of his parent's things, there was a wooden bench at the foot of the bed, a music box on the bureau, a lamp with a fringe, a rocking chair at the window, and books neatly lined up on the shelves like toy soldiers. Next to the lamp stood a picture of Rasa and a man dressed in a soldier's uniform. She had a veil over her head. They were both smiling.

Raymond didn't want to leave the room and Rasa's things, but he was worried that she might sneak up the stairs and find him there, so he hid under the bed. Eventually, the room fell into darkness. The stairs creaked as Rasa climbed them, and then the room brightened with a golden glow. The bed creaked when she sat. She took off her shoes and stood. Her skirt fell to the floor. The bed sagged a little when she lay down, and then the room became dark again. Gradually, Rasa's breathing grew louder and deeper. Raymond rolled out from under the bed and the floor made a noise that sounded like a groan.

"Is that you, Peter?" Rasa murmured. She sighed, and the even breathing returned. Raymond rose and peeked at her face. Her cheek was white like snow. He leaned over and kissed it, pretending he was kissing his mommy. Rasa smiled. Her scent reminded him of toast.

The moon was gone and the sky was light on the horizon. As Raymond looked out the front window, he ached for his family. He wondered what would happen to him. But whatever happened, nothing was as important as his beautiful Rasa, who kept him company in her sleep, and didn't know she was his friend.

CHUPACABRA MOON

Dale T. Phillips

Catherine stood on the rocky beach, looking out over the expanse of gray-green ocean, but also keeping a wary eye on the man moving her way. She didn't like being close to people. There were a few sightseers in the distance, so she felt no danger from the man, only annoyance at having her solitude disturbed.

The wind blew her hair every which way, another reason she liked being alone out here. Normally her hair covered the ugly facial scar, and she hated the reactions of strangers who caught sight of it.

The man was headed right towards her, so she turned to go. She had only gone a short distance before he came up, breathing hard. *Had he run to catch up with me? Boy, was he going to be disappointed.* She didn't even bother turning away, as she usually did. Best to get this over with. Let him get a good look, and he wouldn't be able to leave fast enough.

Instead, he astonished her. "Hi there. My name's Jared. I've seen you out here before."

She knew he'd seen her scar, but his gaze had moved on to the rest of her face. This was unprecedented. She didn't know how to react.

"Sorry to run after you, but I was afraid you'd leave before I could talk to you."

"I have to go," she said.

"Why? Are you afraid to talk to me?"

Now she turned the scarred side away. "What do you want?"

"Can't we just talk, like two regular people?"

"I'm not used to that."

But she had stayed, and talked, and found herself liking this tall, thin young man. She accepted his invitation for coffee, and noticed that he didn't seem to get flustered or embarrassed for himself when other people stared at her. He treated her like she was a normal girl, and she liked that. A lot.

They met again, and again after that. He took her where she wanted to go, mostly away from other people, but also to a few public places. He hadn't asked her about the scar yet, which most people did. Another point in his favor.

When Catherine found out he was a photographer, she almost stopped the relationship. She didn't like cameras, much like she avoided mirrors. But it was so nice not to be alone anymore. She let her feelings develop. She let him take her to bed, though she insisted the lights stay off. Later, she told him about the accident which had claimed her parents and left her with a ruined face and psyche. Three weeks after that, he proposed to her, and she accepted.

Catherine fingered the slim gold band as they rode in the taxi. Married by a Justice of the Peace at City Hall, sure, but married just the same.

She smiled at Jared. "Who's this person we're going to see?"

"The guy who can make things happen. I need a stake to get my business going."

"You don't want me along for that."

"Yes, I do. You're my lucky rabbit's foot."

She smiled at the thought. How could a rabbit's foot be lucky, if the rabbit hadn't been able to keep it?

They were taken to a tall building with a huge marble lobby. They rode the elevator to the sixteenth floor, and sat waiting for half an hour. Then they were shown in to a large office, where a man in a suit stood looking out a window.

"Have a seat," he said, and they did. He turned and crossed his arms. "I've looked over your proposition. That's a lot of money you're asking for."

"It's a sure-fire investment." Jared was sitting forward in his chair. Catherine had never seen him so intense.

"I wouldn't put it that way. A photography business is risky, at best. And your history is, shall we say, a bit checkered. That was some bad shit in L.A."

"That's all in the past," said Jared, waving his hand in dismissal. "I'm a married man now, settled down. I'm responsible."

The man in the suit looked at Catherine. "So here she is."

Catherine touched Jared's hand, a little afraid of the suited man, who seemed to know something about her.

"I keep her out of the limelight," said Jared. "But my work shows what I can do."

The man looked at them both. "You're really going all-in on this."

Jared said nothing, but Catherine felt him next to her, almost vibrating with expectation.

"Tell you what," said the man. "I've got a little project down Mexico way, needs someone on the spot to do a shoot. You go down there, do a good job, prove you can handle it, we've got a deal."

Back at the hotel, Jared was practically dancing for joy. "We got it, oh my god, I can't believe it, we got it." He kissed Catherine. "I told you that you were my lucky rabbit's foot."

"But won't it be dangerous?" Catherine couldn't imagine the two of them driving in Mexico. "He said the village was pretty remote. And you hear in the news about all kinds of horrible things happening."

"Not to worry," Jared said, waving his hand as if brushing away a fly. "First, I speak pretty good Spanish. Second, we've got a guide to drive us."

Catherine looked at him and swallowed. "So this'll be our honeymoon?"

Jared grinned and reached out to touch her face. She forced herself not to flinch. "He'll have a separate room, don't worry. It'll be fine. Trust me.

You're going to love it."

"What happened in L.A.?"

Jared stiffened. "What do you mean?"

"The man said something happened there."

"Oh. Yeah. Well, I'd shoot celebrities and sell the pictures. Some of them didn't like it, and there were a few times we got into scuffles. One day I was after a star, and she was trying to get away and got into a car accident."

Catherine felt the old hollowness. Her voice was barely above a whisper. "Was she all right?"

Jared's face was tight. "No, she didn't make it."

"That's pretty bad."

"Neither did her kids."

Catherine had no words.

Jared went on. "I had to leave after that. Came here, started over. No more stalking celebrities. But I miss the money, which is why we need this."

They were met at the airport by a slim, middle-aged man dressed in white, with dark brown skin like old leather. Running up from his cheek across his brow into the hairline was a long, thin scar.

"Buenas tardes. You are Senor Jared? I am Antonio, your guide."

"All right," said Jared. "You can call me 'jefe,' and this is the senora."

Catherine saw the older man pause as something clicked behind his eyes. They seemed ancient, black, and deep. "Si, jefe."

Catherine looked at her husband. He had seemed to change on their flight, his gestures becoming broader, more expansive. She supposed it was the fact that he had an assignment that would pave the way for his success. For *their* success, she mentally corrected.

The older man turned to Catherine. "Hola, senora." Antonio took her hand, and bowed his head to gently press his lips upon her skin.

She felt a thrill, and responded with her own greeting. She saw Jared smile, but his eyes were narrowed. "Easy there, buddy. She's mine."

"Of course, senor. I was merely being polite and showing respect for the lady. It is how we do things here."

"No problemo," Jared said, giving the older man a light slap on the back. "You just remember who's the jefe, and we'll get along bueno."

Catherine saw the older man wince, and hoped Jared hadn't offended him. He nodded and smiled, but Catherine saw that his black eyes were hard. "Si, jefe."

Jared's smile was broad. "I like the sound of that."

Antonio took their two bags and brought them out to the car. Catherine looked in the front seat.

"Is that a machete?"

"Si, senora," said Antonio. "You never know what kind of trouble you may encounter." He smiled, and Catherine was reminded of a nature show about crocodiles she had seen. They had a smile like that, and she shuddered.

They stopped for lunch in a small village with a market. Antonio told them to walk around and stretch their legs while he took care of some business. Jared said he would get some photos, and he was soon absorbed in snapping dozens of pictures.

Numerous stalls were set up, with brightly colored wares. Jared and Catherine strolled along and looked at the straw goods; the pottery; the leather shop; the food vendors; assorted jewelry. Twice Jared tried to bargain for something that had caught his eye, but the sellers did not speak English, and shook their heads at Jared's clumsy attempts at Spanish. He finally settled on an exquisite, hand-tooled leather belt with silver-colored conchos and buckle.

"Look at this," he crowed. "Thirty bucks. And this is real Mexican silver. I can probably sell this for three times that when we get back."

Catherine was happy that he was happy. She was enjoying herself, loving the exotic locale, despite the assault on her senses. She felt a tug on her sleeve, and turned. There was a short old woman with one milky eye, saying something Catherine couldn't understand.

"What's she saying?" She turned to Jared.

"I can't make it out. Probably just an old beggar that wants some money."

Catherine opened her purse and reached inside to get a few bills.

"What are you doing?" Jared's voice was harsh.

She froze. "Giving her a couple of dollars."

"Are you nuts?"

"What do you mean? We can afford it."

"That's not the point. You give her some, and every damn beggar in this town is going to follow us around. Put the money away. Jesus."

Catherine swallowed. She didn't agree, but didn't want a fight right out here in front of everyone. She closed her purse and shrugged her shoulders at the woman. The woman turned her face to Jared and spoke some words, making a gesture with her hand. She spat.

Jared laughed. "I think she just cursed me."

"Don't talk like that," Catherine said. She was frightened. "Can we go now?"

"Sure. Let's go get something to drink."

They left the marketplace and crossed the street to an open cantina. Inside was slightly cooler than outdoors, ceiling fans slowly revolving overhead.

Jared went to the bar. "Dos cervezas, por favor. Frio."

The bartender frowned as if he didn't understand, but then smiled. He reached into a cooler while Catherine made her way over to a small table and sat in one of the carved wooden chairs. Jared sat in the other, and the bartender came with two bottles of beer and two glasses. He set them down and went back behind the bar.

"See?" Jared smiled as he took a long pull from the bottle. "They pretend they don't understand most of the time, but when there's money involved, they comprende all right."

Catherine looked at the bottle. "I thought I'd mentioned I don't like beer."

"One time won't hurt you. Probably the only cold drink they've got in this dump, and safer than the water."

She poured the beer into a glass and took a tentative sip. The sharp taste made her grimace.

She set down the glass. "So what is this event

you're supposed to photograph?"

"The guy said it's the time of the chupacabra moon. The chupacabra is some kind of monster that roams the countryside, attacking livestock, mostly. The name means 'goat-sucker.' When the moon is right, supposedly, the people put out a sacrifice, a tribute, so the thing won't attack their animals."

"You're kidding."

"I swear, it's what the guy said. No matter. I'll get some great pics anyway. Should have a lot of local color."

"I'm still worried. Anything could happen."

"Ah, don't be such a Nervous Nellie. I can handle anything out there." He eyed her glass of beer and picked it up. "If you're not going to drink this, I will."

Back in the car, Catherine and Jared sat in the back, watching the scenery. They stopped from time to time so Jared could get some pictures. It was a long drive, and Catherine dozed in the heat.

"Would you like to hear a story, jefe?" Antonio said from the front.

"Sure, spin us a yarn."

Antonio began a long tale of Quetzalcoatl, which he said was a symbol of his people. He drew it out, taking his time as the miles rolled past. He went on with another when he had finished the first, his voice weaving a spell. Catherine got a sense of a timeless place, where traditions mattered, and the people endured.

They arrived at their inn at dusk and got two adjacent rooms. Catherine was appalled at the state of the place. Bugs skittered across the floor, and there was no air conditioning, just a fan.

"This is horrible," she said. But no one heard her, for Jared had gone outside to take pictures. She stayed in and watched the shadows grow long as night came.

An hour later, Jared came through the door as frantic as she'd ever seen him. He paced back and forth in the room. "My god, Cath, you have to see it. All these people, and some of them have monster masks on. It's crazier than a Day of the Dead parade. They really buy this chupacabra shit. They staked out a goat, a real live goat, and now they've all gone home."

All during dinner, Jared couldn't stop his chatter. He seemed ready to burst out of his skin. When they returned to the room, he had barely closed the door before he took out a small package.

Catherine watched him. "What's that?"

"This is supposed to be the best weed anywhere," he said, holding up a joint. "They mix it with peyote."

She was stunned. "I didn't know you did drugs."

"Take it easy. I just need something to relax me. My heart's still racing."

"Isn't that dangerous?"

He had a faraway look in his eye. "This is an *adventure*. We're on the trail of something big."

Catherine certainly hoped so. If she was going to put up with bugs, drugs, and stifling heat, there should be some reason.

He puffed away and stretched out on the bed, humming to himself, lost in his world. As the smoke got thicker, she almost gagged.

"What's wrong?" Jared seemed annoyed.

"This wasn't how I pictured our honeymoon."

"I know, but it's going to get better. Come here and try some of this. It'll mellow you out."

"I don't want to. It smells horrible."

"Come on, live a little. It's incredible. The light changes. It's so beautiful."

She gnawed her lip, and weighed the likely argument in her mind. She edged over, and he sat up and patted the bed next to him. She obeyed, and he handed her the glowing splinter.

"Take a big drag, and hold it in your lungs."

She did so, but coughed it out as the harsh smoke burned her mouth and airway.

Jared laughed. "Now try it again, and hold it in."

"I can't."

"Do it."

She took a toke, and he suddenly clamped one of his hands over her mouth and nose, and the other on the back of her head. She couldn't breathe, and struggled, but he kept up the pressure. Just when she thought she'd pass out, he took his hand away, and she choked as she gulped for air.

He laughed again. "That's the way."

Catherine staggered up and crossed the room, holding onto the dresser for support. She was stunned that he'd almost smothered her.

Jared had lain back down. "Now just enjoy the buzz."

Her mind raced, but soon things slowed and grew fuzzy around the edges. There was a strange high-pitched sound in her ears. The past few days of Jared's behavior flipped by her consciousness like a deck of cards. She remembered something that tugged at her mind.

"Jared?"

"Mmm?"

"When we went to see that man. The one you wanted the money from? He seemed like he knew me somehow. Why is that?"

Jared giggled. "Maybe he saw your photo."

"What photo? I don't let people take my picture."

His voice was slow, dreamy. "I did. Shot you before I met you. From far away. Like when I was getting celebrity shots. Used the telephoto lens. Got you looking just right."

"When was this?"

"Couple months ago."

"And you showed my picture to him?"

"To a lot of people. You're famous, Cath. *Lonely Girl Looking Out to Sea*. That photo got everyone's attention, made them notice me. Made me some money, too."

The last pieces of the puzzle fell into place for Catherine. "It was my scar, wasn't it? That's what caught people's attention."

"It's a nice picture, that's all." But she caught the defensive tone in his voice, and knew she was right.

"And when you got noticed for it, you came to meet me," she said slowly. "You wanted the picture to stay yours. You even married me to make sure of it. And to show me to that man, so he'd know you were serious. This was all about your career."

"Hey, Cath, take it easy."

"You used me."

"Things just happened. I didn't plan it all like that. And it's not like you had a lot of other offers."

She stared at him. Stupid: she had been so stupid. Who could love a woman who looked like she did?

She started to cry, ever so silently. At some point, she drifted off.

Catherine woke to a clatter of noise from outside. She opened the curtain, and saw the light of dawn.

Jared stirred. "What's going on?" His voice was thick.

"I don't know. People are out in the square."

"The chupacabra! Shit, we gotta get out there. Quick, get dressed."

"I don't want to go out there."

"Oh, come on. I need you. Let's go."

She shrugged. She couldn't stay in the room forever.

As they dressed, Jared spoke. "You know I dreamed about the chupacabra? It was running in the moonlight. How crazy is that? This place is so amazing."

Catherine didn't tell him her dreams. She had been back on her beach, alone . . . happy.

They went downstairs and out into the crowded square. Jared grabbed her hand and pushed his way through the throng, so that they were standing on the edge of a cleared space. There was a wooden post with a frayed rope, and what seemed like red-and-black trash all around. Catherine couldn't figure what she was seeing at first, and then she recognized that it was the bloody carcass of an animal. She felt faint. Jared was snapping away.

Antonio came up beside them. "The chupacabra took his tribute."

Jared brayed a laugh. "My god, you really do believe it."

The older man looked at him. "You do not? How do you explain this?" He gestured to the gruesome spectacle.

"Some other animal. There's jaguars in the jungle, right? Probably something like that."

Antonio shook his head. "This is not the work of a jaguar."

Jared smirked. "Okay, it was the boogeyman. This was some show, though."

"It is not over. The chupacabra will come again tonight."

"This is unreal."

Catherine just wanted to leave this place, but understood that they would stay here until Jared finished his project. It could be days. Then the reek of blood and opened entrails hit her, and she slumped against Jared, ready to vomit.

"Is the senora all right?"

Jared laughed. "Yeah, she's probably just hungry. I'm starving, myself. Let's go get some breakfast."

After eating, they went back to the room and

napped. When they awoke, Jared reached for his drugs, and Catherine managed to excuse herself. She grabbed her purse and went downstairs, and discovered that behind the little inn was a shaded courtyard. She sat by herself and cried.

She saw the flicker of a shadow and instantly stopped her tears, looking up in the expectation of seeing Jared. But it was Antonio who sat beside her.

"Are you feeling better, senora?"

"Yes, thank you."

"Do you mind if I smoke?"

She shook her head. This man, almost a stranger, gave her more consideration than her husband. She felt anger rise within her at how Jared had violated her privacy and then used her image and her own person to get what he wanted. But what could she do about it?

Antonio lit a slim cigarette and blew a smoke ring. "You did not care for the spectacle?"

"I don't like it when a living thing is sacrificed to a monster. It's fine for everyone else, but the thing being torn apart feels all the pain."

He nodded. "There are many monsters in the land, and we do what we can to keep them from harming everyone. But I think you know what it is like to feel pain, eh? You stay apart from people. We share that, a bit."

Catherine drew a breath, and it came spilling out. "I found out my husband married me because of this scar. I don't think he ever loved me, but he took a picture of me that got him some notice. I guess some people just like to look at terrible things."

Antonio studied her. "Some things may not be as terrible as you think. What is inside a person matters more." He held out a thin case of cigarettes. "Would you care for one, senora?"

"I don't smoke," she said in reflex. The she smiled. "But yes, I will try one."

She put one in her mouth and Antonio lit it for her. She inhaled lightly, and coughed. She kept at it until she could hold the smoke in without coughing.

They sat for a time before Antonio spoke. "Your husband wants to go out tonight with his expensive camera. He wants to take pictures of the goat being killed. He says he can do this from a distance, even at night, and can prove the chupacabra does not exist. This is very dangerous. The people of this village, they do not want their life here to be seen by others. They are angry with your husband and his photos."

She looked at the older man, who seemed to understand her more than her own husband. "That is his mission, and he won't stop. He cares nothing for the people here, or what they want. He will violate their privacy, just like he did mine."

Antonio nodded. He stubbed out the last bit of his cigarette. "It is a risk, to go out during the chupacabra moon. This is an ancient land, and anything can happen."

Catherine's mouth was a tight, straight line. "Accidents do happen, especially when people don't listen to reason. I wouldn't blame anyone or make trouble if something... unfortunate were to occur."

"Stay inside tonight, senora." He stood up,

dusted off his pants, and tipped his hat to Catherine as he walked away.

Jared came down for supper, his eyes red and wild-looking. "Let's go get dinner. I could eat a horse."

During the meal, he rambled on about where he was going to sell the story and pictures, maybe even to television. He said he was going to be famous. Catherine sat and listened, serene at last, and impervious.

"You're awfully quiet tonight," he said, jabbing a fork at her.

"I've got a lot to think about."

Jared smirked. "Like what?"

"What life will be like back in the States."

"It's gonna be awesome. You'll see. Everything's going to be great after tonight."

She said nothing, but quietly agreed.

He left her at dusk, taking his camera and giving her a kiss on her unscarred cheek. She lay on the bed with a book, hearing the noise from the crowd swell and gradually fade away. She read for a while before going to sleep.

In the morning came a knock on the door. The corridor was crowded with people. There was the innkeeper, Antonio, a policeman, and people behind them whispering.

"Yes?"

"Senora, we have terrible news. Your husband. He was killed by the chupacabra last night."

She put a hand to her mouth. "What?"

The man shrugged. "It was foolish to go out during the chupacabra moon. He was attacked."

Catherine tried to look shocked. Antonio spoke up. "I think the senora should be alone now."

They murmured assent. "Of course. Our sympathies to you. Please let us know if you need anything."

She closed the door on them and rested her head against the wall.

An hour later, Antonio knocked. "I am sorry to come to you in your sorrows," he said. "But there are arrangements to be made. Shipping the body, for example."

"No need," said Catherine. "He had no family. Would they bury him here?"

"Perhaps it could be done. I could help with that, if you would like."

"I would like that very much. You know I don't speak the language, and I don't know how things are done here."

"There is the matter of the death certificate, which you will need to take back with you. As to the cause of death . . ."

"Could it just be put down to 'animal attack'?"

Antonio nodded slowly. "That seems best. This is a quiet village, and they would not like strangers coming to disturb things. I think senora will find the people here will all tell the same tale, of a careless turista who went out when he should not have."

"I appreciate the consideration. I wish I could show my gratitude somehow."

"There *is* the matter of personal effects," said

Antonio. "His camera, a watch, his wallet . . . that belt he bought in the market. Some of the items have blood on them, I'm afraid."

"Keep them," said Catherine. "They have no sentimental value for me. Perhaps you could see that they help others to get through this tragedy. I think I have enough to get home."

Antonio bowed. "I will take care of things, then. Let me know when I can drive you back."

She thanked him and shut the door after he had gone. She squared her shoulders and began to pack, humming a tune.

In the corner of the room, a tiny scorpion scuttled across the baseboard.

COLOR HIM CRAZY

Stacey Longo

Bart James sat among the spectators in the courtroom, listening to the prosecutor's opening statement outlining the case against Bart's little sister. She'd stabbed her boyfriend to death, then barbequed his corpse and eaten it. The prosecutor seemed to think it was an open-and-shut case. In his heart, Bart glumly had to agree. His sister Etta was done for.

The details of the case made Bart sweat. Did crazy run in families? Could *he* be criminally insane, too, his inborn tendencies just waiting for the right time to coil and strike?

He thought of their father, Hank James. Dad had had a wicked sense of humor, the kind of guy that thought it was funny to name his oldest son Jesse, his middle boy Bartles N., and his little girl, Etta. Dumb? Sure. Ensuring that his children would be teased by classmates for life? Without a doubt. But crazy? Bart didn't think giving one's kids ridiculous names quite qualified.

What concerned Bart the most was that Etta was now his second sibling to be arrested for murder. Two years earlier, Jesse had been sent to jail with four life sentences for kidnapping and murdering women. It had been quite the scandal, and Bart had wound up canceling his daily paper when the trial was going on, just to avoid the headlines. It turned out that Jesse had liked to cruise the bars in downtown Boston dressed as a cop, pick up young college girls who were too drunk or too unfamiliar with the city to find their way home, and drive them out to deserted areas outside of town. Then he'd strangle them and dump their bodies in the Charles River.

Jesse had been caught due to his own insanity, Bart had no doubt. Jesse had grown so fond of the Halloween-store cop costume he wore to go hunting for women that he'd taken to wearing it all the time: while mowing the lawn, grocery shopping, even to church. Witnesses had seen some of the girls leaving with a costume-store cop; it hadn't taken long for the police to find their man.

During the time that Jesse was on his serial-killer spree, Bart had seen very little of his older brother. Jesse had gotten increasingly harder to talk to over the years, and Bart was often frustrated trying to have a conversation with him. It was difficult for Bart to discuss politics or the economy with a man who insisted that the world was going to shit because "purple." How could Bart argue against that? No, he and Jesse had not been close, and Bart hadn't visited him once in jail since his conviction. Etta mentioned going to see Jesse only one time; when Bart had asked how their brother was doing, Etta'd said "He's convinced his cellmate is Ronald McDonald, working undercover to expose the prison beef industry. So I'd say he's about the same." They'd discussed it no further.

Now Etta was on trial, accused of a heinous murder. Bart's sister sat at the defendant's table, her short, spiky blue hair clashing with her sedate brown suit. He should've seen the warning signs that Etta was losing her grip on reality. Last year, their mother had been diagnosed with an aggressive form of lung cancer, and withered away in a matter of months. On her deathbed, Mom had laid a frail hand on Etta's.

"Sweetheart," their mother had rasped, and Etta had leaned in to hear her dying wish clearly. "You *really* need to do something with your hair," Mom had said, then wheezed and died. Etta had taken her mother's last words solemnly to heart, and had chopped off her silky caramel locks in favor of the spiky blue cropped helmet she wore now.

That was probably not a normal reaction, Bart thought. *The wheel was still spinning, but the gerbil was slowing down even then.*

Etta had started dating Simon Place about two months after Mom had died. Things seemed to be going well, from what Bart could tell. Bart and his wife Mina only saw his sister every other month or so. He was shocked one night to get a call from Gary Hatcher, the James family's longtime attorney, announcing that Etta had been arrested. Bart had kissed Mina goodbye the next morning and made the hour-long drive from his home in Middleborough to the police station in Lowell. Etta had been indignant when he'd finally gotten in to see her in her holding cell.

"He *proposed* to me, Bartles, can you *believe* it?" Etta had stormed. Bart had been confused. Wasn't that a good thing? Apparently not.

"I've been stuck with that floozy blues singer's name all my life. You think it was easy? Guys singing 'I Just Want to Make Love to You' as soon as they met me? And *then*, when that bitch re-released 'Something's Got a Hold on Me'? Every day I had people serenading me. Every *day*. Don't get me started, Bartles. You have no idea." She'd held her hand up, apparently forgetting that her brother had been named after a popular wine cooler, and had taken some ribbing of his own throughout his life.

"So what happened?" Bart had asked.

"I told him there was no way I was going to marry a guy with the last name 'Place,'" she'd said, throwing her hands up in frustration.

"Huh?" Bart had said.

"Jesus, you too? Simon didn't get it, either. Etta Place? Are you kidding me?"

"Still not getting it," Bart had said, frowning.

"Don't you ever read a book? Or even watch old movies? Etta Place was only a huge prostitute that hung out with Butch Cassidy and the Sundance Kid, jackass. I am *not* going to trade my stupid drug-addicted blues singer's name for a big ol' turn-of-the-century hooker's name. No thank you," she'd said, as if this explained it all.

"Sooo . . . you decided to slit his throat and cook him in Bull's Eye Original instead?" he'd asked.

"Well, yeah. I was hungry," Etta had shrugged.

Brother to both a serial killer and a cannibal. That was Bart's lot in life now. He wished he was home so he could talk to Mina, get her take on the situation. Was she worried at all that he might be secretly nuts? After all, two out of three of the James children had turned out to be murderers. Good lord, what if he and Mina had had children? Not that this was even an issue: Bart had always been the sort who preferred pets to people. But what *if* . . .? How would he have explained to his children that their aunt and uncle were both killers—not to mention the inherent danger to his imaginary kids. *They* could've been victims. Bart shuddered at the thought. He felt like he'd narrowly escaped a terrible fate.

But *had* he escaped?

Bart didn't know if insanity was genetic. Sure, he'd known growing up that his brother Jesse was weird. His friends' brothers had never painted portraits of JFK on the sides of *their* houses using nothing but motor oil and feces. Clearly, Jesse had been an oddball. But Etta? She'd seemed mostly normal.

Mostly normal . . . but not quite, he had to admit. Hadn't Etta once dressed up as Hannibal Lecter for Halloween when she was only ten? Sure, that wasn't so bad, but her insistence that she eat nothing but liver and fava beans for the entire month of October had been odd. Bart supposed that it had been a little strange for a fifth grader. No self-respecting kid that age voluntarily chose to eat liver. And for 31 days in a row, no less.

But why had his parents indulged his nutty siblings? Dad, gone now ten years, had always enjoyed a good joke. When Jesse had proudly led his family outside to see his huge JFK oil-and-feces display (and, Bart had to admit, it *had* been impressive in its detail) Dad had roared with laughter. The JFK portrait faced Ed Swann's house, and Ed was something of a ball-buster. Many a night Ed had called the cops on the Jameses to complain that the kids were playing their harpsichords too loudly or that they were setting off fireworks at midnight, in February, in a residential zone. If nothing else, Ed Swann was a bully and a killjoy, and a giant likeness of John Fitzgerald Kennedy made of fecal matter facing Ed's living room window was sweet justice. Dad hadn't been bent out of shape at all that his oldest son had smeared shit on the side of the house. One good downpour later, and it had washed away anyway. No harm done.

Bart smiled at the memory of his father. He often wished he could go through life with such an easygoing attitude. His dad had never seemed to worry about mortgages, or that weird noise the car was making, or whether or not the company he worked for was going to survive the recession. Life had thrown curveballs at Hank James from time to time, but he'd just let it all roll right off his back. Bart envied him even now.

His mother, Penelope James, had been another

story. She'd been the disciplinarian in the family, and had blown up at Jesse when he'd painted the presidential poo portrait. Jesse had been forced to eat his dinner with a toothpick while keeping two clothespins clamped on his earlobes every night for a week after that incident. Mom had been *tough*. But, theoretically, it should have taught the kids discipline, right? Then why hadn't his brother and sister learned the importance of that one big rule: thou shalt not kill?

Bart couldn't figure it out. Mom had been firm, but fair. Whenever the kids behaved well or got good grades, she made sure they were equally rewarded. Bart still remembered their mother surprising them with handmade bracelets made out of raccoon hair and teeth. Mom had caught, killed, skinned and de-boned the critters herself. *Nothing in the world quite like a mother's love,* he reflected thoughtfully.

Sure, maybe Mom's methods had been a little unorthodox. Probably making Bart eat a floral-scented candle after he stole a Twinkie from the grocery store had been a little extreme. Or forcing Jesse to wear a dress and wig to school after he'd dropped the f-bomb at the dinner table. Hoo, boy, that had taken years for poor Jesse to live down. The school football team had beaten him up every day for a month after that little fiasco. But was forcing your daughter to scrub the kitchen floor with her toothbrush after spilling flour really *that* excessive? Bart was sure other kids had gone through similar punishments. In any case, it hadn't hurt the James children any, and probably, in the long run, had made them better people.

Bart listened to the prosecutor wrap up his opening arguments. Bart didn't know why Etta was even bothering to fight the charges; the evidence clearly pointed to her, and she'd admitted to Bart himself she'd done it—not that he'd told anybody that. Family was family, and he wasn't about to testify against his little sister. He sighed, folded up the newspaper he'd been reading whenever there was a sidebar, and got up. He was attending the trial to support his sister, but it had already been a long morning. Surely she'd forgive him if he slipped out early to go have lunch with Mina.

Bart left the courthouse and walked down the street to the Walgreens at the corner. He bought a box of Crayolas and some Beggin' Strips, then waited at the bus stop to catch his ride home. He should be there by 12:30, just enough time to have a lazy meal with Mina, discuss his thoughts, and ride back downtown before the afternoon court session started. *Perfect*, he thought.

Mina was lying in bed when he got home. She didn't flit about the house much during the day, and sometimes it seemed to Bart that she spent most of her time just waiting for him to come home. He had some guilt about this, but continued to run his daily errands. After all, nobody wanted to be in another's company 24 hours a day, right? *Familiarity breeds contempt*, he reassured himself as he placed the Beggin' Strips and crayons on the kitchen table.

"Mina?" he called out. "I'm home!"

Mina casually sauntered into the kitchen

without acknowledging that he was there. She was probably steamed at him for leaving so early this morning without so much as a kiss goodbye. "Don't be mad, babe. I had to run out early; I told you that," he explained as she sat. She watched him with wide brown eyes, but didn't respond.

"Come on. I really need to talk to you about something. I'm worried—well, as you know, both Jesse and now Etta have done some pretty awful things. Are you—do you worry at all, and be honest here, that I might be crazy, too? What if I suddenly went nuts and started threatening people? Killing them, even? Would you still love me? Would you—leave me?" He choked out these last words, burying his head in his hands, both eager for and fearful of what her response might be.

Mina moved over to his side, gently nudging his obscured face.

"Woof," she replied softly, licking his hands. He stared into his wife's face, her chocolate coat shining from the brushing he'd given her the night before. She wagged her tail. "Woof," she repeated again, solemnly.

Well, that was a relief.

Bart kissed Mina sloppily on the cheek and began serving lunch. He placed four Beggin' Strips on a plate for Mina, then selected blue violet, burnt sienna, tan, and screamin' green for his own plate. They munched on their respective lunches in silence.

"At least we have each other," he sighed, finally. Mina looked at him and panted, letting her tongue loll out. "Don't do that," he chastised her gently. "You look ridiculous."

THE SLEEP ARTIST

Vlad V.

If Wanda Warby failed, the baby would die. Maybe it would be cancer, or heart disease, or some other awful thing that would drain the smile away from the innocent's lips, until the baby passed. Wanda was a considerable woman with a considerable will, and she resolved not to fail. She peered through the slats of Miguel's crib, leaning forward on the chair, watching him toss and turn in his teddy bear pajamas. His exhausted little face was out of place on a seven-month-old child.

She felt a stir of anger. The doctors had resorted to drugs to get him to sleep, but those hardly worked at all. Wanda had sensed the psychic imbalance emanating from baby Miguel the moment she'd picked him up. His energies were all off. Skewed. The doctors were way out of their depth here. This aggressive type of insomnia couldn't be cured by modern medicine.

Six months of tests and they still don't know why Miguel won't sleep more than a few hours a day.

Miguel's parents, both good Catholics, lower middle class, were sleeping in their bedroom down the hall of their dingy apartment. Andres worked for the Highway Department. Julieta stayed home to raise the baby.

They were at their wits' end. Desperate, placing their faith in their god, Andres and Julieta had agreed when Father Sullivan suggested that perhaps someone outside their church might be able to help them with this particular problem; Sullivan was one of the few who understood what reality was really like.

Wanda had worked with the father before when he reached spiritual impasses. In Miguel's case, the higher-ups in the church wouldn't sanction an exorcism, because he didn't fit the necessary criteria. Miguel was too little to speak, never mind in languages he shouldn't know. Since he could only babble, he displayed no knowledge about occult practices. Perhaps most of all, he displayed no physical aversion to sacred things, such as the cross, prayers, or holy water.

Wanda wasn't a particularly religious type—it was all too political for her taste—and she believed that there were many different paths to God anyway . . . which was the beauty of being human. She also believed that there were even more paths to His counterpart . . . the danger of being human.

"You're a spiritual healer?" Andres asked from the doorway of the nursery as Wanda settled herself in the stiff wooden chair in front of the crib.

His sun-browned face was drawn, sallow. Julieta's hand clutched his arm, digging her nails in, her teary eyes glistening.

"Sort of. I'm what they call a Sleep Artist. I interpret a sleeper's energies and try to determine what might be harming them."

People with strong religious beliefs had resisted Wanda in the past, because it could be difficult for them to understand what she did, but Andres just nodded, resigned. Wanda felt her shoulders relax. Father Sullivan had already softened them up.

"Thank you for coming, Wanda. Father Sullivan spoke very highly of you."

"Si. Gracias, senorita," Julieta said. "I hope you can . . ." her voice trailed off, and she started to cry.

Wanda gave them strict instructions then: "This may be an intense session, so if you hear me, don't be alarmed. Please, whatever you do, don't disturb us until the morning. It can take hours for me to get into the proper state of meditation, and if you disrupt me, I may have to start all over again tomorrow night. That wouldn't be good for me or Miguel." She smiled warmly.

Let them think I'll be meditating. That's something they can understand.

Meditation didn't have anything to do with it. Not here, not tonight.

Wanda and baby Miguel were soon alone, and Wanda's grip tightened on the chair as she took stock of the room. Energy had begun to hum in the back of her skull, like a plucked guitar string she could feel but not hear. The crystals on the floor at Wanda's feet had been laid out in an intricate pattern. She never knew what the pattern was going to be until she was actually making it, her hands guided by a power she didn't fully understand. Tonight, it looked a bit like a dream catcher. On the window, the smear of lamb's blood was already drying to black. More blood was drying on the door and the vents as well, to keep the thing in Miguel from escaping.

The white urn she'd made on her potter's wheel now rested on the floor next to her with its lid off. It was etched with every holy symbol she could think of: Christian, Buddhist, Muslim, Jewish, all the way back to Roman, Greek, and Sumerian. Wanda never knew who she was going to be dealing with, so she used as many symbols as she could, all crammed together on the surface of the urn. It had to hold whatever she came back with.

That humming suddenly grew in strength, and the lamp with a scarf thrown over it to dim the glow went out. The nightlight flickered.

"And hello to you, too," she whispered, reaching down into the duffel bag beside her chair and pulling out a few white glow sticks. She shook them, cracked them, then tossed them about the room. They landed softly on the carpet. The ethereal beings could mess with electricity pretty easily, but for some reason, disturbing chemical reactions seemed beyond their reach. They were clever parasites, and she thought of them as ticks or leeches growing fat on spiritual blood before slithering off through the higher dimensions to slumber for a decade or a century, only to wake and breed before seeking out another host. Always twisting the Good into the Dark, innocence into something awful. It was tastier that way. It was how they made their victims *ripe*.

Miguel whimpered, tossed, kicked. He appeared asleep, but he wasn't really sleeping. The doctors had discovered that with their brain wave tests. He wasn't hitting deep REM sleep often enough; hardly at all, really.

Wanda leaned forward in the chair, rubbing her hands together, the flab on her upper arms rippling. Tonight, she'd chosen jeans and an oversized blouse to accommodate her considerable form. It could be a long night, and she needed to be comfortable.

"Let's get this party started, sweetheart."

The nightlight went out, but the soft white aura of the glow sticks resisted the change. The lump that was baby Miguel sat up. He looked at Wanda, and Wanda looked back. Miguel stood up as if his body was on fast forward, his limbs jerking up as if he were a puppet. It was an unnaturally quick motion for a seven-month-old who couldn't even crawl yet. Sitting one moment, standing the next. His dark little gaze never left Wanda's. The hollows of his sunken eyes challenged her; the lines on his exhausted little face were shadowy cracks in the aural glow.

Wanda waited, a patient warrior biding her time. Her enemy upped the ante, and Miguel began to rise off the mattress, hovering one, two, and then three feet over the sheets.

Wanda was unfazed.

Miguel's arms jerked straight out to the sides, his chubby legs slamming together, as if he were being crucified. Seconds ticked by. One of Miguel's arms snapped just above the wrist, and the *snicking* sound of his bones breaking turned Wanda's stomach. His little hand now pointed straight up at the ceiling. Miguel's eyes widened with pain, and for a moment his mouth moved, but nothing came out. Then he pulled in a shuddering breath and shrieked in such agony that Wanda's first instinct was to leap from the chair.

She didn't move.

Miguel's other arm snapped, and this time his hand was pointed down. His face morphed into uncomprehending anguish. His legs twisted at the knees until his feet pointed backwards, as if a giant's hands were ripping apart a chicken wing. Oh, how Miguel screamed!

Wanda began to sweat. Inside, she trembled at the savagery, and bile rose into her throat. Outside, nothing showed on her face.

The force wasn't done with baby Miguel. His legs began to rotate until they popped out of their sockets at the hips and hung noodle-limp over the pale blue sheets.

The baby screamed. The parents slept.

Wanda leaned forward, her eyes hot, her hands gripping the arms of the chair to keep her rump planted firmly where it was, safely behind the pattern of crystals separating her from that evil force.

"Aw, poor little thing," Wanda cooed. "Haven't you ever tangled with a Sleep Artist before? I'm the best in the business, honey."

The illusion shattered, and Miguel was suddenly lying back in the crib, unharmed, tossing and turning, where he had been all along. The screams and the breaking bones had been meant only for Wanda; demons were experts at twisting reality. The lights didn't come back on, however.

"And the score is Wanda, one; Demon, zero," she taunted.

Wanda forced a smile. The thing had expected her to fold, to stagger out of the room, winded by the scream caught in her throat. The humming in the back of Wanda's mind grew to such a pitch that it tickled her eardrums and teeth, like a swarm of bees buzzing around in the back of her head. A shriek spewed out of from that sound, reptilian, maybe something else; she couldn't tell. She winced in pain as her stomach turned again.

Maybe not too much arrogance, then. Just enough to tease it out.

Wanda removed two misshapen stone pyramids from her duffel bag, forged from shiny obsidian. Misshapen, malformed things that represented the demon. Their tips were very sharp, and Wanda placed on one each arm of the chair, then rested her palms over them so that they poked her clammy skin, but didn't quite pierce. She closed her eyes and focused. A tingling began to pulse in her forehead, and she drew in long, slow breaths until her psychic energy was beating to its own mysterious rhythm. The energy in her flesh vibrated like a tangible thing, wanting to get out, her physical self keeping it formed to the necessities of her biology; her living body was simply a vessel. She tingled from head to toe, and then she projected her energy out of herself, imagined that she was stepping out of her own skin. This wasn't far from the truth.

She was a nebulous entity now, a crackling force attached to her physical body only by a very thin thread of psychic energy. She glided over the crystal pattern before her feet, absorbing the protective power as though it were a suit of armor. That awful humming was abruptly muted, but she'd have to make sure it didn't fade completely, otherwise she could lose it and the demon could flank her.

Miguel's mind was populated by dim memories of warmth and milk, love and amniotic existence, strange sounds and the deep rumble of his parents' voices, memories through which Wanda moved effortlessly. She quickly reached the black wall where his memories stopped, and mentally, she frowned. She sorted through the memories again, slower this time. No smudge. No smear. No black nightmares through which the parasite had initially entered. This wasn't right. Usually, Wanda could find the exact moment of infection (she found the word "possession" technically inaccurate, even though that's what movies, books and even some churches often called it), like a shadow was dimming one moment of memory, but not the one before or after it. She filed through Miguel's memories a third time, but found nothing.

Weird.

"Let me in," she commanded. Her voice was loud to her ears, and yet Wanda's lips barely moved, hissing out little more than a whisper. "Let me in!"

No response.

"Fine. If that's the way you want it, parasite."

Back in the chair, Wanda's palms pressed down on the tips of the pyramids, piercing her skin, sinking into flesh. Blood beaded down the warped slopes. The humming intensified as the parasite grew excited by the lure of blood, before it caught itself. Wanda's energy crackled with a smile, while in the chair, a slight upturn of the lips creased her slackened face.

But where are you? Wanda wondered. Again, she went through Miguel's memories, but came to that flat black wall, behind which was nothing, for the child had had no consciousness yet. *But the demon is here.*

Wanda summoned all the memories of all the parasites she'd ever destroyed, casting them out into Miguel's mind like fishing lines, ready to yank them back at the slightest nibble.

"What's wrong, Nameless? Is wittle itty bitty demon afraid of an overweight, middle-aged dreamer? Is that it?"

Hubris. So often their tragic flaw. Use their arrogance against them.

The humming increased, a rumble within it this time. The demon's voice, angered by the memories of its brethren being slaughtered by a clucky old hen like Wanda Warby. The black wall, the starting point of Miguel's conscious mind, faded into gray, resolved into an image of a gloomy city street at night, rain splashing down on a few cars parked along the sidewalk that looked as if they were from the 1920s. This was the demon's memory, when it had last possessed (*infected*) a human and disguised itself as a person. Miguel was now acting as the bridge between Wanda and the demon.

The demon was accepting her challenge, but Wanda hesitated. The fact that the black wall of non-memory in Miguel's mind was acting as the door into the demon itself meant that Miguel had been infected at the very moment of inception, because no memories preceded it.

How is that possible? And why? she marveled. And then, a cold finger of doubt. *Can I handle this?*

She should retreat. This parasite might not be one of the soul-suckers she was used to battling, but something different. Maybe something worse. This issue should be sent higher up the food chain in the loose organization that stretched across the globe and constituted the human force of Good. It certainly wasn't the arena for a Sleep Artist.

But Miguel was running out of time, and Wanda needed to know more. She took a deep breath, steadied herself, and then moved into the demon's mind, slipping back through time, to a memory not her own.

Rain splashed down on dark buildings, washing clean a line of cars parked along the sidewalk. Wanda studied them. Boxy cars with boxy windows, white wheels, elongated front ends and bug-eyed headlights. A 1927 Model A Ford. A Lancia Lambda. A Bugatti Type 35. Across the street, a Scotch Wool and Hosiery store next to an R.H. Hogg's Provisions and Grocery. The lettering on the windows was antique, sculpted in fonts she associated with a time that had long since passed.

A car chugged out of a side street, circled in the road, and then parked at the curb. Two finely dressed gentlemen in suits got out. They didn't see Wanda, because she hadn't taken a form yet. The men hurried around to the back doors and ushered two ladies in long, sleek dresses out into the night, holding umbrellas over their heads. Their dresses were backless, with bodices slightly bloused, both in muted colors, one with a white fabric flower on one shoulder.

The group vanished through a door, and Wanda suddenly appeared behind them—distances were meaningless in memory, much as they were in dreams. The four had entered a small, well-lit café serving two bedraggled customers, both men, who studied the group a bit too intently from the padded stools along the counter.

"Say, Mary, how are you tonight?" the gentlemen leading the group asked the woman behind the counter.

"Oh, you know, Ed. Slow nights these days," she winked. "I'm still looking for a pip who's plenty rugged, so if you see one, make sure you let me know. I haven't seen my rascal of a husband in over a year."

"Don't be glum, Mary. You're a real ring-a-ding-ding," Ed replied.

Mary and the group laughed as Ed slid right by the counter and around the corner into a short hallway, then led the boisterous group into the men's bathroom. Inside, Ed opened the janitor's closet. Beyond was a clear path to the back wall through all the cleaning supplies.

"Come on, kids. The giggle juice won't pour itself," Ed smiled as he ushered them inside. He knocked on the back wall.

A peephole slid aside, and a single reddened eye glared out. "Yeah?"

"Trip for biscuits."

The back wall opened to a set of stairs leading down to a narrow subterranean passage, along which they moved single-file to another door. Another peephole, but this time when it slid aside, music poured out.

"Password."

"Mickey, Mickey Finn," Ed replied.

The door opened to reveal a large, smoky room. A band flung their tunes over sweaty dames and gents dancing frantic swing. People knocked elbows at the bar while sucking down brightly colored drinks, and others gambled at a roulette wheel, or eyed each other slit-eyed in games of poker.

My god. I'm in a speakeasy. It must be the Prohibition era.

Wanda marveled at the fashions, the shiny table tops, and the long filters on peoples' cigarettes. The place was vibrant, and Wanda recognized it as a hub, a place where the demon had once spent quite a lot of time, resulting in a multi-layering of memories. What she was experiencing wasn't necessarily what had really happened; it was only what the demon and its human host had perceived everyone else to be experiencing. It was fair game for all kinds of manipulation, and luckily, memories were liquid things, could be manipulated, misinterpreted, or poorly remembered. Herein lay her skills. She had wiggle room.

But why had it picked this arena for their

confrontation?

It was time to take a form. Wanda chose the blond woman on Ed's arm with the pink dress and the white flower on her shoulder, sliding into this physical caricature of the demon's memory. Now she was in. She could interact and be seen. She tasted the smoke and the scent of whiskey in the air, and felt the dress, soft against a thin body that wasn't hers.

She listened for the hum, but it was gone, lost in all that music. This made her uneasy. She swallowed hard and surveyed the crowd. Any one of them could be the parasite. The pudgy man staring at her over his poker hand. The roulette dealer. The sweaty, braless woman in the sheer dress, swing dancing, not knowing or not caring that the dark rings of her nipples were sticking out.

Someone pinched her bottom and she screeched and whirled around to peer into a dark, handsome face. A mischievous grin played on the man's lips.

"It's been too long, muffin. Let's say you and I find some place more comfortable."

"I think not," Wanda replied.

"What are you being so stiff for? Ain'tcha glad to see me?" The smile faltered, and he looked hurt. "I love you. Don't you love me?"

Wanda pulled back and let the memory surface, so that she wouldn't project too much of her own psyche into things. Time to take a backseat.

"You know I do, Ray-Ray. It's just that things are so complicated right now."

"Sophia, I'll marry you right here. And then I'll tell everyone."

So I'm Sophia in this when. Nice name. I like it.

Sophia giggled and looked at him slyly. "But Ray-Ray, don't you need to ask your boss for permission? You can't even hit the street without his say so."

Ray-Ray's dark eyes smoldered, and his jaw clenched. He grabbed her wrist hard enough that it hurt and yanked her close, so that they were nose to nose. "I'll be the boss in this town soon enough, baby doll, and don't you forget it."

Wanda felt his grip on Sophia's wrist, but right now Sophia was a little breathless, a little frightened, and more than a little turned on.

"You're handsome when you're angry, Ray-Ray. I kinda like it."

"Come on. There's a room in back." He started pulling Sophia away, muscling through the crowd, pushing people a little when they didn't move quickly enough.

Ed saw what was going on, hurried through the crowd, and stepped into Ray-Ray's path, squaring his shoulders for a fight. "Say, what's the matter? Who is this clown, Sophia?"

"You'll keep your trap shut if you know what's good for you, pal," Ray-Ray replied, shouting over the music. He drifted away from Sophia and slipped a hand inside his suit jacket. An image of a gun, a polished steel revolver, flashed into Wanda's mind.

Sophia gave a little laugh. "Oh, boys, let's not be daft. We're all here for a little fun, aren't we?"

"She's my dame, pal, so shove off while you still can," Ray-Ray warned.

Sophia shrugged. "It's okay, Ed. We're old

friends. Come on, Ray-Ray."

And then she was pushing Ray-Ray away before things went sideways, leaving Ed looking crestfallen and puzzled before he receded into the crowd. Ray-Ray took control again and dragged her along, Sophia hurrying in short steps because of her heels. They rounded the bar, passed the bathrooms, and headed toward a door at the end of the hall.

Ray-Ray tried the knob, growled when he found it locked, and then kicked it open. Among towering crates of whiskey, rum and gin, the couple going at it on the little cot cried out in surprise. The man looked up, his hair tussled, while the woman covered her little breasts with both hands.

"Say, what's the big idea, Ray-Ray?" the man yelled. Ray-Ray strode in and slapped him across the face. Hard. The man's head rocked, the woman screamed, and then Ray-Ray had the man by the hair and was dragging him out the door. "This is how you repay the boss? Ain't you on the clock?"

"I'm sorry, Ray-Ray! I didn't mean to—"

Ray-Ray dropped him in the hall, cocked his leg back, and kicked him in the balls. The man's eyes bulged as he gasped for air, folding into a fetal position. Ray-Ray turned back into the room, but the woman was already gathering their clothes, her eyes locked on Ray-Ray in total fear. She scampered through the door with their clothes pressed to her naked body, and Ray-Ray shut the door behind him with the heel of his shiny black shoe. It didn't close all the way, but he didn't care.

"Don't forget to write," Sophia laughed.

Wanda felt a surge of repulsion . . . and yet,

there was a surge of something else in Sophia that bled over into Wanda's mind, something she hadn't felt for a very long time. Then Ray-Ray was on Sophia, his lips pressed to hers, and Wanda gasped, surprised at how good it felt. He shoved her down to the bed, desperate, pulling her dress aside even as she fought her way out of it. Wanda felt the warmth of Ray-Ray's cock through his suit pants as Sophia started to rub it. He yanked his belt off and flung it aside; she pulled down his pants and his thick member sprang out, a massive, throbbing, uncircumcised thing.

Wanda bit her lip and thought, *Oh my.*

Then they were naked and Ray-Ray was on top, ramming into her. Sophia moaned. Clutched Ray-Ray's muscled shoulders, digging her nails in. Wanda wanted to moan too, but fought it. He swelled all the way in, filling her. Sophia whimpered.

"It's good, isn't it? You like it, don't you?" Ray-Ray whispered into her ear.

No! Wanda thought.

"Yes!" Sophia said.

Ray-Ray thrust harder. Faster. Wanda bit her lip. This level of intensity was something completely new.

"You like it, baby doll. Tell me you like it."

"Yes! Yes I do!" Wanda cried through Sophia's mouth. His breath tickled Sophia's earlobe, and she gave in. She couldn't help it. She shuddered in time with every one of Ray-Ray's violent thrusts, his handsome face hanging over her, the sweat of his brow curling his hair. Far away in Miguel's bedroom, Wanda squeezed her thighs together and climaxed.

Ray-Ray was off her and pulling his clothes on as soon as he finished.

"Leaving so soon? How about another go?" Sophia purred.

He grunted. "I got business."

"Can I come?"

"I can't have no dame biting at my heels."

Sophia sat up, grabbed Ray-Ray's belt, and pulled him against the bed. "What if I say please? You know how I get when I see that old iron of yours."

"Old? I don't think so. Pretty soon I'll be the boss of this town. You'll see. Then I can get old."

"With me at your side?"

"You know it, dollface."

"I don't believe you." Sophia pouted and rolled away, facing the wall.

"Oh, come on. Don't be like that. I already told you I love you."

She looked back over her shoulder. "Then let me tag along. I won't get in the way. I promise."

Ray-Ray sighed heavily. "You stay behind me if things get hot, got it? Stay close to the door. And keep your trap shut. I can't have no dame running her mouth when she ain't supposed to."

Sophia leapt out of bed and started dressing. "Sheesh, Ray-Ray, I'm no dummy. I can behave, when I want to." She smiled, and Ray-Ray grunted again. "Where we going?"

Ray-Ray grinned. "This is the boss's club. We're already here."

He led her through a door behind the bar, the bartender stepping out of their way without a word, into another storage room, and then to another secret room hidden behind a wall of shelving. Four men looked up from where they sat around a table, squinting through the smoke curling up from their cigarettes. Three of them were sharply-dressed men with expensive hats and watches; the fourth was much younger, in his early thirties, with penetrating green eyes and a shrewd look about him. The top few buttons of his black dress shirt were unbuttoned, the sleeves rolled up to his elbows, his suit jacket hanging limply over the back of his chair. Papers had been spread haphazardly over the table, several with lists of names, districts, and public departments on them.

One of the older men stood up, beaming at Ray-Ray and clasping his hand when they went to shake. "Raymond! Say, I was beginning to think you wouldn't show."

"I wouldn't dream of missing it, Mister Piebold," Ray-Ray said. His voice had changed. It was soft, respectful. No menace in it at all.

"Mister? We're all friends here, Raymond," Piebold laughed. "Who's the looker?"

"This is my girl, Sophia."

Piebold looked her up and down, extending his hand. "Enchanted. If I wasn't on my third wife . . ." He winked.

"And if I wasn't with Raymond here . . ." Sophia winked back, and the men laughed and started making room for them at the table.

Piebold hustled Ray-Ray to the younger man with the green eyes. "This is the money man I was talking about, Chester. Raymond Pound, international investor extraordinaire. Raymond, meet Chester White."

Ray-Ray's eyes fell on the younger man as they shook hands. "So you're the man I've been hearing about, the puppet master pulling the strings of politics?"

"You're too kind. I prefer to think that I influence the voting booth for the betterment of the American people."

"By rigging the game?"

Chester laughed. "You were right, Piebold. He is a sharp knife."

"I told you," Piebold said brightly.

"You have no idea," Ray-Ray said.

Chester poured a glass of whiskey and handed it to Ray-Ray. "Please, sit down. Listen to what I have to say. It's all on the up-and-up. You'll see."

"You're a hard man to pin down, Chester. If it's all straight talk, why this secrecy?"

He shrugged. "Some people don't like my politics." They sat, and Chester began shuffling through the papers. He looked at Piebold. "You're sure he can be trusted?"

"Yes, yes." Piebold waved a dismissive hand.

"I'm risking my neck by coming out into the open like this."

"In a secret room, in a joint like this? That's out in the open?" Ray-Ray smiled.

"He's a good Joe. It's all aces. You'll see," Piebold said.

Chester studied Ray-Ray for a long moment, then said at last, "Okay," and began laying papers out in front of Ray-Ray, one by one. Wanda saw they were typed by an old typewriter, and she noticed the date atop one of them: April 2, 1923.

"I know you're a busy man, Raymond, so I'll get straight to the point. This here is a list of public employees and department heads that support us. This list is our base of, shall we say, more influential supporters. You can see it's a very, very long list. And that's just the beginning. This here is a redistricting plan based on voting histories of local neighborhoods that we believe will also support us, despite the potential retaliation from the Family. Brave citizens, if you ask me."

"And what you want from me is money to fund your political interests? Is that right?"

Chester folded his hands and looked at Ray-Ray. "I mean no offense here, Raymond, but Piebold told me about your father and your uncle rotting up in Springer Penitentiary for minor hooch offenses that shouldn't be offenses at all. Is that what justice is?"

"No."

"No, indeed. Who likes Prohibition? Nobody I know. The Temperance movement started with good intentions, but it's made criminals of us all." Chester stood and began to pace. "I do need money, that's a fact, but what that money will buy isn't just to get people into the voting booth. It's for protection, too."

Ray-Ray scoffed. "Protection? From who?"

Chester stopped and looked at Ray-Ray. "The mob. If Prohibition ends, the mob's racket ends with it. Millions of their dollars go spinning down the crapper. We're three years into Prohibition, and look what it's cost us. Hooch provides a steady source of income for the mob, but leads to other crimes, like gambling and prostitution. Gang wars. Money laundering." Chester's voice fell to a whisper. "Innocent people caught in the crossfire, or extorted. Fathers and mothers. Children, even. You see, if anything has consolidated the mob's power in this country, it's Prohibition." His voice began to rise. "Now you pay more than gold for what used to cost a pittance, and the only way to get it is illegally. All we've done is strengthen a criminal element into an organized force to be reckoned with. That's why it has to end. We have to cut the funding out from under them and deal them a death blow while we still can." He jammed a finger down on the papers. "I can end Prohibition in a year; two at most, Raymond. I see the way! It'll start here, in this city, and then the rest will fall like dominoes. We'll move from town to city, city to state, state to country, and once we're in Congress, we'll fix what's broken."

Chester's eyes were blazing now, and Ray-Ray was moved.

"Gentlemen, I believe I've heard enough," Ray-Ray said.

"So you'll help? You'll join us?" Chester leaned over the table in anticipation.

"I'll write you a check right now." Ray-Ray reached into his suit jacket and removed the revolver, pointing it casually at Chester White. Sophia gasped. Piebold and the other two old men froze. "You said it yourself, kid. If Prohibition ends, then so does my boss's monopoly in the hooch business. Can't have him losing millions, can I?" Chester swallowed hard. Ray-Ray waved Piebold away. "Good work, Piebold. Way to grease the skids. Now go."

Piebold leapt up and scurried out the door, knocking his chair over in the process. Sophia's breath was coming in short, breathy gasps.

"You're an amateur, kid," Ray-Ray said to Chester. "You come into a joint like this with no bodyguard, no one to pat me down for an iron? Who do you think owns this place?"

Chester's face had gone pale, but when he spoke, his voice was strong. "Piebold told me it's his cousin's building."

"Ain't that sweet."

"I've always been a trusting man. Human decency will prevail, Raymond, if that's even your real name. One day, it will prevail."

"If you say so."

The gun boomed and Chester White staggered back against the wall, blood spreading across his chest. One of the old men grabbed for the whiskey bottle while the other lunged over the table at Ray-Ray. He shot them both, one after the other. The bottle rolled off the table and shattered on the floor.

Sophia's breasts were heaving at the sight. "Oh. Oh," she breathed. "They'll hear us, Ray-Ray! Someone will—"

Ray-Ray slapped her across the face and she fell out of the chair. "Over all that music? The walls are too thick, you dumb broad." He tucked his gun away and slid a knife out of his suit jacket. "But just to be sure, let's find out."

Sophia's eyes went wide. "It's me, Ray-Ray. It's *me*."

"Sorry, dollface. The Boss said there can't be no

witnesses." A hard lump was forming in Ray-Ray's pants as he stood up.

"Wh-what about P-piebold?"

"He's one of us."

Ray-Ray grabbed for her foot. Sophia kicked, but Ray-Ray grabbed her ankle and dragged her across the floor toward him. He leapt on her, slashing her breasts, slicing right through the dress. Wanda felt the searing pain. Sophia screamed and clutched her chest. Ray-Ray pinned her head to the floor and lopped off an ear. This time she shrieked.

"Shut—" Ray-Ray cocked his fist back and then slammed it across her temple. "Up!"

Sophia went limp. Wanda felt the dizziness, barely able to hold on to the memory. Ray-Ray resumed carving, lopping off the other ear and putting it into his mouth. He began to chew.

Wanda couldn't take it anymore. She leapt out of Sophia's body, her psyche hovering in the air over the table. Ray-Ray looked right at her, and Wanda felt a chill.

I've got my eye on you, Wanda, my dear, Ray-Ray spoke into her mind.

It sees me! she thought.

Do you think this is my first rodeo, dollface? You did well in there, letting me fuck you like that. You're just a lonely old woman who needs a little love, aren't you? Poor, sweet Wanda Warby who hasn't had a man—

Shut up!

Robbed of the most basic pleasures in life by your addictions. You're only human. What's a little skin now and then?

SHUT UP!

Ray-Ray reached down, dipped a finger into Sophia's blood, and wrote on the floor: Wanda, 1. Demon, 1.

Wanda didn't withdraw from the demon's memory—she was thrown out with such force that her physical body shuddered as her energy slammed back into it. Her hands slipped off the pyramids, which tumbled to the floor. She sat there, her bosom heaving, her face damp with sweat, her crotch still wet.

She was a large and aging woman who hadn't been with a man in a very long time, not since she'd given up her abusive husband and her addictions and embraced the Good.

Once, Wanda had been a fat and lonely child, a victim of bullies, a loser. She had hated herself. So she ate . . . and gained more weight. Years later, in her late twenties, she was finally able to lose most of the weight after countless bouts with one diet or another. She became attractive; pretty, even. She knew men, lots and lots of men, and her therapist wondered aloud that she might be a borderline nymphomaniac.

But still, there was something missing, some void that had never been filled . . . until the day she met Henry, the love of her life. He introduced her to drugs, and they got married, higher than kites. Wanda found she loved getting high on anything and everything, preferably on combinations of things. Quaaludes, weed, cocaine, and booze were an especially nice mix. Crack and anything else wasn't bad, either. And the *sex* on some of it . . . oh my!

Henry turned out to be little more than a low-level street thug, however, and he was handy with his fists, especially with his women. *Women* being plural.

When Wanda finally saw the light and got clean, ditching her no-good husband, she swore off everything that had brought her down the wrong path, including sex outside of a loving relationship, because even that could be a form of addiction. Everything except food. What was the harm in that?

The void within her had never really been filled in the first place, only covered over, and it came creeping back, until she was fighting the same battle she'd fought thirty years earlier as a young woman. Wanda had come full circle.

The parasite had somehow sucked the loneliness and her sexual addiction from her head and used it to its advantage, like a chess player cornering the king. It had picked that arena so it could seduce her, weaken her with a little . . . skin. A rush of shame and revulsion warmed Wanda's neck.

She looked at the crib, where little Miguel was tossing and turning. She hadn't even commanded it to reveal itself. She'd been so completely obscured by the demon's illusions that she'd folded like a freshman recruit. So quickly and easily the demon had compromised her; seduced her; made her sin.

She looked out the window at the flat black night, at the lamb's blood on the window.

She could still leave, and summon someone else. Maybe she should contact one of her higher-ups after all. Maybe this really wasn't a job for a Sleep Artist.

But we're so few now, and spread so thin. The Dark is surging, growing stronger every year. How long will it take for reinforcements to get here? How much longer does Miguel have before he's terminal? Days? Hours?

"Get a hold of yourself," Wanda whispered. "You're a pro. One of the best."

A scraping sound rose from the humming in the back of her mind. The demon was laughing at her.

She needed to think. Why had the Dark sent one so powerful against a baby?

Prohibition; and with that, organized crime . . . mob subversion to ensure that liquor remained illegal and they could reap the consequences. The date! She'd seen the date on one of Chester White's papers: April 2, 1923. White had said he could end prohibition in one to two years, and he seemed to believe his own words, but Prohibition had dragged on until 1933, a decade after his assassination at the hands of a demon-possessed mob hit man. A decade that had secured organized crime's position in American life. A decade that had catapulted its savagery and its power into the highest offices in the land. And it was still there, wasn't it? Only now it had gone international, growing into a malevolent parasite that sucked decent people dry.

Could Chester White have stopped all that? Could his political wiles have changed history before organized crime got too ingrained in modern society?

The potential in Chester White had been defeated by the flaw in Ray-Ray, which the demon had used to its advantage. The Dark would've loved for Prohibition to keep trucking along forever, increasing human misery, subverting mankind to its basest flaws and desires, and seducing souls away from the Good all the while.

My god. Chester White was a fulcrum! Wanda sat back in the chair. The epiphany hit her like a truck. *An Aristotle. A da Vinci. Tesla. Einstein. One of those special people who come along and pivot mankind toward its divine potential, fundamentally changing things for the better.*

She'd never known anyone who'd encountered a fulcrum before. She'd only read about them in coded history books that could never leave the hidden, subterranean classrooms of her secret school. Anecdotal evidence at best. Again, she realized she was out of her league, and it came with a tremor of fear, but then her eyes focused on the crib, staring hard at Miguel. If Chester White had been a fulcrum, did that mean Miguel was a fulcrum, too?

He's so young. The Dark wouldn't go after him at this age, unless maybe he's someone like a . . . she hesitated to say it. *Prophet?*

Rumors had been circulating for years that the Dark Seers were gaining their powers back, after being temporarily defeated at the end of the Dark Ages. Their loss allowed for the Renaissance and the reopening of mankind's ability to think and reason freely, as it should be. Had the Dark Seers prophesied Miguel's rise to greatness, and intended to stop it while he was still so fragile?

There could be no waiting now. She couldn't leave this task unfinished. She was a Sleep Artist, and one of the best. She needed to find her inner strength and rally.

Her head spun with the implications, but Wanda felt a bizarre sort of honor that *she* was the one fate had chosen to do battle against such a powerful being. Wanda swallowed hard, collected her pyramids from the carpet, and pressed her palms down on them in a new place, drawing fresh blood.

"Time for round three, *dollface*," she growled.

Wanda walked fast along the sidewalk and refused to look back.

"Hey, Wanda Wobbles, what'cha wobbling so fast for?" John Boyd called from behind her. After years of torment, she'd recognize the class-bully-and-general-asshole's voice anywhere.

She cringed, rolled her eyes and heaved a sigh, flipping her middle finger up over her shoulder. Now she did look back with a smile, just to make sure he got the point. Her smile faltered. John's minions, Tony and Tim, were walking home from school with him through the tree-lined streets of suburbia, and they weren't more than thirty feet behind her.

Between her and them, Marvin Millson was trying not to put out the special scent that seemed to say *hit me*, which every bully since preschool had been able to sniff right out. He was a year behind Wanda, in the sixth grade, a quiet kid with thick glasses and a clutch of comic books in his hand. He looked at the pavement as he walked, motoring right along, catching up with her. She couldn't blame him. Sheep were safer flocking together when wolves were around.

"Why're you so fat, Wobbles?" Tony called.

Her face flushed red and she clasped her books to her chest and kept walking.

"That's a real nice dress, Wobbles," John called. "Looks like your mom made it out of a couch."

"I kind of dig it. It looks good on her," Tim said. "If you need something to sit on."

"She's big enough. Let's try it. Let's sit on her." Tony shouted. He ran in front of her and stopped short on the sidewalk. He was taller than Wanda, but half her size. She bumped into him hard, knocking him on his ass, and kept right on going. John and Tony roared with laughter, and even Marvin smirked a little, although he quickly tucked it away, his face going blank.

Wanda willed her feet to go faster. *I will not run. I will not run,* she told herself. The sight of her clumsy steps and the bouncing rolls of the weight she hated so much would only entice them. She couldn't outrun them anyway.

The bullies stopped to put their heads together and light their Chesterfield cigarettes from a book of matches. Wanda and Marvin exchanged a look and sped up.

"C'mon, Marvin. Let's hurry. I don't want to deal with those jerks today," Wanda whispered.

They picked up the pace, their red brick middle school fading from view. Wanda and Marvin turned the corner and began walking alongside Kingman

Pond. Wanda looked back. The boys had fallen from sight.

"Go right home, Marvin. Don't sit by the pond to read today, okay?"

Marvin nodded. Wanda crossed the street, went up her driveway, and hurried inside. The smell of fresh-baked blueberry bread greeted her, but she didn't go into the kitchen to get some. She peeked through Mom's lacy curtains hanging in the living room. Marvin was gone, having ducked through the bushes along the footpath that weaved along the shores of Kingman Pond. John and his friends came down the road and stopped at the path, puffing and pretending to be long-time smokers because they surely thought they looked cool.

"Keep going, you jerks," Wanda whispered. John's house was just down the road, and he didn't need to use the trails around Kingman Pond to get there.

Tim snapped a dead branch off a tree and used it as a sword, poking it at the other two boys. They laughed and batted it away, taking heavy drags off their cigarettes. Then, one by one, their eyes swiveled to the path. John shrugged and then ducked into the greenery, vanishing after a few feet. Tony and Tim followed.

A bad feeling washed over Wanda. The trails on this side of the pond were fairly secluded, and with the beach on the opposite shore, no one was likely to come along and save poor Marvin if the boys decided to rough him up.

She rushed across the street to the path, but then stood there indecisively. Surely Marvin wouldn't stop to read his comics when those jackals were around. Would he? But he had a habit of taking off his shoes, putting his feet in the water, and then lying back to read before going home. If he stopped, it'd be his own fault. She'd told him to go right home.

She thought of the blueberry bread Mom had made, waiting for her on the counter. Her mouth watered a little. Then she felt bad for thinking about blueberry bread, because it meant John and his friends were right about her—she ate too much. It made her want to cry, so she went down the path, telling herself that this counted as exercise (and way back in her mind, that maybe it would allow her to have an extra slice when she returned). She moved through the bushes to the worn, narrow footpath winding along the shore.

It wasn't long before she saw John, Tony, and Tim creeping up on Marvin, who, like a big idiot, had stopped to read after all. He was lying in an open space along the shore with a comic book held over his face. Marvin had a way of engrossing himself in those stupid stories. He didn't see John and his friends sneaking down the path. They hunkered behind a fallen tree not thirty feet away from him. Wanda stepped into the reeds along the shore and her shoes sank into the mud, soaking her feet. She swore and stooped down so that the bullies wouldn't see her.

John picked up a small pebble, grinned at his friends, and then chucked it at Marvin. It sailed high over his head before splashing into the water. Marvin jerked his head up, and the boys snickered with laughter. Wanda frowned. Tim waited for Marvin to fall back into the book, and then threw a larger stone in a line-drive. It streaked right over Marvin's nose, struck the comic book, and yanked it right out of his hands, knocking it into the water.

"Hey," Marvin cried, leaping up and rescuing it from the pond. He stood there with a look of utter dismay on his face while water dripped from the pages, his eyes swiveling over to John and his friends. "You guys are a bunch of assholes!"

Tony stormed out from behind the tree and stomped down the path, John and Tim in his wake. There was no way Tony was going to take that kind of guff from a dork like Marvin, and a sixth-grader no less. "What'd you call me, shitbag?"

Marvin's bravery faded and his face went pale. He grabbed his comics and hurried away down the path barefoot, leaving his shoes behind. Tony picked up a sneaker and hurled it at Marvin's back. It struck him in the shoulders with a smack, and Wanda cringed.

"Did you forget something, Marvin?" he cackled. Marvin bent to pick it up.

"Hey, don't go. Don'tcha want your other shoe?" John laughed.

Marvin vanished down the trail with the bullies in hot pursuit. Wanda followed, praying the boys wouldn't turn around and see her. But they were intent on Marvin now, and there was blood in the water. They grabbed sticks and small rocks, flinging them over Marvin's head or just to the left and right of him, making him cringe and duck, laughing whenever they got a reaction. Mostly, they just wanted to scare him, but they cackled like hyenas whenever one of them "missed".

Soon Marvin was hunched down with a comic book shielding his head, stumbling down the path. The salvo continued, and the sticks got bigger. John whipped one as thick as his forearm. It spun awkwardly through the air before slapping Marvin across his butt cheeks.

"Leave me alone!" Marvin howled, clapping a hand to his ass and jumping away. The boys roared. Another stick sailed from Tim's hands, bigger than the last one, and hit Marvin's hand, skinning a knuckle and ripping the cover of a comic book.

"C'mon, guys! I'm sorry! Stop it, please!" Marvin cried.

"You hear that, boys? He's *sorry*," John said.

They'd come to a place where the trail was just a step or two away from the water's edge. John bent over and wrestled a rock the size of a softball out of the dirt.

"Watch this," he grinned at Tony and Tim.

He cocked his arm back, aimed at the sky, and let it fly in a lazy arc. Wanda froze. The rock rolled end-over-end through the air, on a course that would bring it right over Marvin and into the pond, splashing him with water. It hit a tree branch instead. The lazy arc turned into a plummet, and it struck Marvin right on the top of the head with a wet, hollow sound that made Wanda want to puke. Marvin toppled over and fell face-down in the pond, his comic books falling around him in a loose flock.

The boys stopped. Wanda stopped. For a moment, nothing happened, but then Tony and

Tim looked at John.

"I . . . I was j-just trying to splash him. That's all," John said.

"You killed him, John!" Tony said, his voice going high-pitched with shock and fear.

"I didn't mean to! Don't tell anybody! Promise me you guys won't tell anybody!" John screeched.

Tony and Tim backed away, then Tony cut and run straight into the woods, and Tim followed him. John stood there indecisively for a moment, looking toward his friends to Marvin, and back again, then he ran after them and didn't look back.

Wanda hustled up to the body after they'd gone. Marvin wasn't moving. His body bobbed facedown in the knee-deep water, tiny waves licking his cheeks. She could see his glasses resting on the sandy bottom a few feet from his head. Already, a massive lump had formed on the back of his skull, and his blond hair was smeared with either mud or blood.

I need to get help. I need to tell someone.

But something anchored her feet. She couldn't move. John and his friends were just so popular, and Wanda wasn't. John played basketball and Tony was a star player on the football team.

A thought bloomed from somewhere down deep: *maybe this is my chance.*

If she kept her mouth shut, then maybe they'd start to like her. They'd have to. She'd tell them about what she'd seen if they didn't.

I can keep a secret, she'd say. *I won't tell, so be my friend. Or else.*

A frog jumped into the water from a cluster of lily pads.

It wouldn't be easy, she knew that. John, Tony and Tim would be suspicious at first. At worst, she could stop them from picking on her. She'd just threaten them with the truth. But at best, maybe, just maybe, she'd convince them that she was all right. Maybe they'd invite her to parties. Maybe even . . . a school dance. She'd even go with Tim, the ugliest of the bunch. It was better than going alone, or not at all.

Wanda fantasized as Marvin lay there facedown in the water.

He's not going to drown, she thought. *That's crazy. He just got bumped on the head. He'll wake up any moment and collect his comics and then go home. He'll just have a headache, that's all.*

Marvin wouldn't tattle. He never tattled. He took his lumps and tried to forget about them like a good victim. Wanda looked to the mussed hair on the back of his head, to that clump of blond hair.

Don't be silly. That's not blood.

Slowly, Wanda made her way back home. He'd be okay. She just knew it.

But Marvin wasn't at school the next day, so Wanda sank into her classroom seat and stared out the window.

A concussion, maybe. It was worse than I thought, but he'll recover. He'll be back in a day or two.

John, Tony, and Tim were unusually quiet. No swearing. No punching the younger, weaker kids in the hallways. They huddled around a locker, whispering conspiratorially. Tim caught Wanda looking on her way to class, and she averted her gaze, staring at the checkerboard floor as she hurried by.

She went from math to English to history in a daze. Mr. Pensky's lecture on the Revolutionary War was interrupted when Principal Kipp came into the room.

"A moment please, Mr. Pensky," Kipp said.

The two men stepped into the hallway and shut the door, and when Mr. Pensky returned a few minutes later, he was wiping at his eyes. He stood at the front of the room, opened his mouth, shut it, took a deep breath, and then wrung his hands together.

"Class, I . . ." his voice cracked. He swallowed, tried again. "Class, I have . . . some very bad news. This is going to come as a shock, but I'm very sorry to say that—that . . . Marvin Millson is—was—found dead last night in Kingman Pond," he finished in a rush.

A few kids gasped. The rest were big-eyed and silent. John, Tony and Tim looked at each other, their faces blank.

"Oh my god," Wanda whispered. Her heart sank, and she felt a little dizzy.

Mr. Pensky looked at her. "Do you have something to say, Wanda?"

"No, I . . . no."

The other students were looking at her.

"Do you know what happened to Marvin?"

"No. Why would I?"

She gathered her books in a one-armed sweep and headed for the door.

"I didn't give you permission to leave."

Wanda was usually an obedient girl, but right then, she didn't care. She stumbled down the aisle and threw the door open, hurrying down the hallway. Mr. Pensky and the entire class filed out behind her.

"Where are you going, Wanda?" Mr. Pensky asked.

"Do you have a guilty conscience, Wanda?" a student added.

"Wobble away like you did from Marvin, Wanda Wobbles," another cried.

Classroom doors opened ahead of her, students and teachers pouring into the hallway to block her. She turned abruptly to a set of stairs and hurried down to the first floor of the school. Younger students emerged from these classrooms, glaring at her accusingly as they shuffled into the hall.

"Got something to hide, Wobbles?"

"Why didn't you pull Marvin out of the water?"

Wanda whirled around and went for the exit doors, bursting out into the sunshine at the back of the school. The entire student body followed her. A hand tapped on her shoulder and she screamed. It was John Boyd.

"You could've saved him," he said. "But you let him die just because you want to be popular. You're a real scuz, Wobbles. Do you really think I'd ever take *you* to a dance? Dream on."

She was heading across the parking lot to the baseball field, intent on taking the shortcut home. She had to get away, couldn't meet their eyes.

Principal Kipp cut her off, leaning against the fence along the first-base line. "Do you know how badly Marvin's parents are suffering right now? Do you even *care*?"

"Of course I care," Wanda mumbled.

"Then why'd you let him drown?" Tim whispered into her ear.

She jumped. Principal Kipp pointed a finger. "You're a greedy, fat child. You don't deserve to be popular. You don't deserve to have friends."

"I'm sorry. I just . . . I didn't—" Wanda started to cry.

"We'll never like you, Wobbles! You're a real zero," someone spat.

"You should've called the police, Wobbles."

"Why did you let him die, Wobbles?"

"Shut up! Leave me alone!" Wanda shouted.

She reached Principal Kipp and stopped. The student body had her surrounded. There was nowhere to run. They jeered and swore at her, spitting on her as the ring around her grew ever tighter. Wanda turned a slow circle. Eyes accused her and hands reached for her. The students were ten feet from her, then five. Fingers grazed her dress.

"You went home and ate blueberry bread. A whole loaf of it. Did it taste even better after you let Marvin die?" Mr. Pensky asked.

I didn't eat it, Wanda thought. *Not that day. I couldn't. Not after . . .*

It was a small thing, but it was enough. The demon had made a mistake, and now part of her, the much older part that was still sitting in the chair near Miguel, recognized that the parasite had found one of her worst childhood experiences and recreated it for its own ends.

Wanda shivered. She'd been flanked. The protective pattern of crystals at the feet of her physical body was like plastic wrap, when what she really needed was steel armor. A demon gaining access to her memories, then manipulating them so effectively? This wasn't supposed to happen! The danger with all the others had always been the moments just after excision, when she had to wrestle it into the urns decorated with all those holy symbols.

But Wanda was back now, and rallying. Among the crowd of students, she smiled. "That's not what happened."

"You let Marvin die, Wobbles!"

"I'm not perfect, but I did save Marvin that day. I dragged him out of the water and then ran for help. I saved his life." She nodded to herself, affirming the truth. "I saved his life."

Her old classmates stopped, went silent, and then vanished. There one moment, gone the next, as if someone had pressed the 'delete' button. Wanda felt the demon's power ebb, and sensed its surprise.

She summoned all of her energy, faith and power into her voice and shouted, "I command you! *Reveal yourself to me!*"

It was an uppercut to the chin, and now the parasite was on the ropes, dazed. She moved in for the knockout blow.

"Reveal yourself to me! *I command you!*"

A shadow began to form over the pitcher's mound, first as a formless blob, then spreading until it blocked out all of second base, then the infield. Wanda was forcing it to take a form. Wisps of darkness molded into a dozen beetle-like appendages armed with pincers, a scaly black body draped in obsidian chain mail, dozens of round yellow eyes peering from the deep hood of its black robe.

Wanda and the demon sized each other up. It was more cunning than anything she'd ever encountered, yet she walked patiently toward the baseball field.

"I'm here to destroy you, vile thing. Now take your form, or are you a coward?"

A hiss rumbled from its mandibles. "I am Shad'noc, Bringer of Shadows, General of the Infinite Brigade, Destroyer of Angels, *and I will break you!*"

Wanda threw her head back and laughed. The demon charged, skittering forward and crushing the metal bars of the fence under its weight. Wanda stood fast as it swept toward her, its pincers tearing up chunks of earth as it closed the distance. It loomed above her, and Wanda glimpsed a long black throat filled with gyrating white hairs before its mouth crashed down over her psychic body, swallowing her whole.

Energy splashed into energy, and Wanda and Shad'noc plummeted through experience and time, manipulating memory into implements of war, changing realities that once had been, flinging themselves and all they had been, were, and might be at each other. Soul versus soul, human flaw versus human potential, the battlegrounds were always themselves.

1775. Secret messages were captured by a British spy on the eve of the Revolutionary War that would determine the outcome of the rebellion against the Crown. Wanda, as a young farmhand, killed Shad'noc, stole the messages back, and delivered them.

1978. Wanda was living in a crack house, struggling with the addiction that set her hurtling toward the Dark. Shad'noc, disguised as her husband Henry, tried to convince her to stay long enough for an overdose to kill her.

1517. Martin Luther barely escaped assassination on his way to post his controversial Ninety-Five Theses when Wanda alerted him to the man stalking him through the streets of Wittenberg, Saxony.

1990. Wanda stood before the doors of a church, and this time she finally went inside, leaving the love of her life behind, because he was, and always would be, an addict. The act set her, finally, on the path to the Good.

1502. Leonardo da Vinci was seduced by a wealthy merchant's wife, but Wanda switched the poisoned wine at the last moment.

1967. Wanda attended a peace rally, and alerted police to the gunman before he started his rampage.

1348. A merchant knowingly sold blankets infused with the Black Plague, intent on spreading death into Eastern Europe. Wanda caught the disease, and the merchant escaped with his deadly load.

1981. The body of one of Wanda's druggie friends was found in an alley, and instead of reporting it, Henry convinced her to forget about it.

888 B.C. Shad'noc, disguised as a Mayan priest, stood clutching a baby at the peak of a temple, thousands of cheering people clustered around its base. The knife went up and then down, but Wanda stopped the demon's hand.

Good was turned to the Dark in their minds, and the Dark was destroyed by the Good, but always back in time they went, deeper into Shad'noc's memories, Wanda pushing the parasite ever closer to its weakest moment; exhausted, so exhausted, but always striking, driving it back. They battled in many places throughout Wanda's life; in Rome and China, Greece and England, on remote, no-name islands teeming with forgotten peoples, or the crowded streets of ancient cities. In politics and religion, invention and philosophy. Egypt and Russia. Turkey and Brazil. China and Africa.

Wanda attacked with human potential, and the demon countered with human flaw; their faith in both was their armor.

They battled until at last Wanda stood in a great stone room of an ancient building with ornately beaded and dyed tapestries hanging on the walls. A woman dressed in a white shawl bordered with a simple blocky pattern was curled up on a strange-looking bed, little more than an oversized bag of straw. Thin stalks poked out of the fabric here and there.

A wrinkled old woman stood near the bed, and so Wanda took a form by entering her. Now, through the old woman's eyes, she saw the wriggling body of a baby wrapped in cloth nestled close to the woman on the bed.

The mother looked up at Wanda. "I am very worried, Ahassunu. My dreams are troubled. What futures have you seen in yours?"

So I'm a soothsayer in this when.

Wanda let the version of Ahassunu that Shad'noc remembered rise to the surface. "My queen, your son Kubburum will be a greater king even than Gilgamesh, who built the Walls of Uruk and possessed the knowledge of the gods," Ahassunu rasped.

Gilgamesh? Wanda thought. *That's Sumerian. I'm in Sumer! The genesis of human civilization!*

Never had she gone so far back in time and memory before. A few centuries at most, but never back to the beginning of everything. Shad'noc was ancient and powerful indeed, a titan among ants. And where was it hiding? Possessing the mother? The baby?

The queen looked at her critically. "You have foreseen it?"

"I have foreseen it," Ahassunu replied. "Come, my queen. Allow me a closer look at one so blessed. It is not every day that one gets to bask in the presence of divinity."

"You may come forward."

Ahassunu tottered closer. Wanda felt her brittle bones and swollen joints as she moved. It pained her, but her heart was warm nonetheless. Wanda studied the child's wrinkled face. "Truly a blessing. Allow me to hold him?"

"Of course, my old friend."

Wanda bent over the baby and picked it up very gently. "Reveal yourself to me."

"Is something wrong, Ahassunu?" the queen

frowned.

"Nothing at all, Great Queen," the old woman replied, reaching into the folds of her shawl and pulling out a stone knife, its blade honed from obsidian. The queen screamed, but Ahassunu retreated toward the window. "One step, Queen of Shit, and your babe's life ends."

The heavy wooden doors burst open and the queen's bodyguards rushed in, wiry men wielding stone-tipped spears or axes, their wraparound skirts hanging to their knees and held up by thick, rounded belts.

"Stop!" the queen shrieked, and the men stopped just inside the door, glowering at Ahassunu. The queen got to her knees and began crawling across the stone floor, hands out in supplication. "Please, good Ahassunu, I do not understand. Please don't hurt little Kubburum. He's just a babe."

Ahassunu raised the knife, the queen screamed, and the soldiers took a step forward before the queen shouted, "No!"

The blade jammed down . . . but Wanda stopped it just shy of the little one's throat. Ahassunu resisted her. Impossible! She was just a shell.

Hello, dollface, Shad'noc chuckled, and Wanda went cold.

The blade lowered, made a dimple in the baby's cheek. They were both in Ahassunu! The demon was coming right at her, now that her strength was waning. Wanda gritted her teeth and fought back. The blade wobbled over the baby's face. The child opened his eyes and started to cry.

This is how it happened, dollface. The baby died

and it took centuries before even the tiniest seeds of the great philosophies began to emerge. How many souls came to us because of it? From persecution and war? Disease? Racism? Greed? Millions. Doomed millions.

"Not this time," Wanda seethed. "You'd better hope I don't get sent to Hell, demon." And with one quick motion, she turned the knife toward Ahassunu's chest and plunged it into the old woman's heart. Wanda felt the pain, felt the stone slipping between her ribs, slicing into her heart, the breath driven from her lungs. She folded to the floor, placing little Kubburum gently on the stone as her body slumped back against the wall.

Wanda saw it then: a shadow rising out of Ahassunu's body, Shad'noc as it had been at its first possession, when it had been its weakest, inexperienced, having just been born. It was long, skittering and shelled like a centipede. It rose above the body into the air, its mandibles clicking, rows of yellow eyes lining its insectile head.

With Ahassunu's dying breath on her lips, Wanda flung the last of her psychic strength at the parasite, latching onto it in a death grip. It wriggled and gyrated, and she felt its pincers slicing through her brain. But she yanked Shad'noc forward in memory. 888! 1348! 1775, pulling it all the way back to the present, right into Miguel's humble little bedroom in a dingy Boston apartment.

This was the moment she'd been fighting for. Wanda was herself again. Her arms flew up and her pyramids toppled to the floor as Shad'noc screeched and writhed over Miguel's bed, a shadow, a silhouette, an energy, but terrifyingly real. Wanda snatched the urn with one hand, hanging on tight to the demon with the other, tipping the urn so that the lid fell off.

"By the power of the Good, I command you, demon of the Dark! By the power of all that is holy, *I command you!*"

Shad'noc turned in the air, its many eyes peering at her. For a terrible moment she was sure she was going to lose it, that it was going to claw its way back into Miguel's soul even deeper this time, but then it was pulled down toward the urn as if by a vacuum.

It was weakened. She'd done it. She'd battled one of the Ancients and survived. She felt a rush of pride.

The demon slowed as it passed over the urn and was sucked downward, dozens of its little legs frantically treading the air, trying to get away. Then it surprised Wanda, jerking itself past the opening and flying right at her, slamming into her mind. The crafty thing had held one last burst of energy in reserve. Wanda was too stunned and exhausted to fight it off. The delicate urn fell from her grasp and broke on the carpet. She gagged, feeling Shad'noc sink into her soul like a ball of slimy, twisting worms. Then the feeling was gone as it warmed to its new home.

"No . . . no . . ." Wanda whispered, rocking back and forth on the chair.

And you think I'm the one guilty of hubris, dollface? That's the pot calling the kettle black. You weren't chosen by fate. You were chosen by me, and it looks like you bit off more than you could chew, Shad'noc chuckled. Wanda whimpered. *Don't fret, my dear. You're only human. We've been watching you for a long time. You've destroyed so many of us, and your power grows even as you age. You're the strongest Sleep Artist we've ever seen.*

"No!" Wanda cried, but this time, no voice came out. She was now just a passenger on this mystery ship; Shad'noc was steering the wheel.

Miguel was bait, she realized. Her limbs trembled and she felt a deep-down sort of terror; the witch before the fire, the prisoner before the gun, the skydiver with a faulty parachute.

I knew you'd come for a child, Wanda. Ah, what darkly divine missions I can accomplish in the soul of a Sleep Artist, Shad'noc whispered, and quite against her will, Wanda felt a smile pull across her face. Shad'noc flexed Wanda's fingers and took a deep breath. *The Age of Darkness has been foretold; the Apocalypse is here, and you and I will launch the first salvo in the final war against the Good. Buckle up. It's going to be one hell of a ride.*

Shad'noc commanded Wanda's body to stand, and stand it did. It rummaged in her duffel bag for a small notepad and a pen and then scribbled a quick note: *Sorry for the mess. Had to run, family emergency, but I was able to help Miguel. He'll sleep just fine from now on. See you soon!* ☺ *~ Wanda*

It put the note down on Miguel's baby-sized bureau, using a box of infant wipes as a paperweight. Humming to itself, Shad'noc took Wanda's bag, crept out of the bedroom, and then down the hall to the front door. In her car, it rifled through Wanda's mind for directions. Wanda screamed and fought, but she was utterly a prisoner.

Within an hour, Shad'noc stood before a ticketing counter at Logan Airport, clutching Wanda's bag in front of it with both hands. This world had changed so much since Prohibition, and the bustle of the airport and the snazzy technology everyone seemed so obsessed with had it on full alert. It was nervous.

A clean-cut young man in a company vest bearing a nametag that read *Chuck* peered back at it.

Shad'noc tried on a smile, which prompted the young man to ask, "Can I help you?"

"One ticket to Jerusalem, please."

Chuck brightened and looked at the heavy woman with interest, fishing a necklace with a silver crucifix out from beneath his crisp white dress shirt. "Oh, man, I'm so jealous. You're going to *love* it there. I went with some friends after high school. One of those overseas luxury tours? You *have* to see the Old City. It's got the Western Wall, the Church of the Holy Sepulcher, *and* the Temple Mount with the Dome of the Rock, so you get to see a little of all three major religions." His brow furrowed and he lowered his voice. "It's such a beautiful place. It can be a real flashpoint though. Too bad there's always so much fighting going on over there."

"Yes. Too bad."

"Oh, and don't forget about Hezekiah's Tunnel. Really, it's a-*ma*-zing. Are you going for business or pleasure?"

"Pleasure. Most definitely pleasure."

ACKNOWLEDGEMENTS

Insanity Tales was a collaborative effort between the five authors involved. Each author submitted their stories to the others, and provided feedback, critique, and insight to each other as the anthology developed. There were many late nights and rewrites involved. One of us required copious amounts of chocolate.

Writing can be a lonely business without a good support team. These authors work together regularly in a cooperative effort to improve their own writing and the writing of each other to produce the best final product possible. Each author brings his or her own perspective, skills, and experience to the group, resulting in an extended collective knowledge base that none of the authors would have achieved on their own.

If you are a writer, consider working collaboratively with other like-minded folks whom you respect. Personally, we think of our collaborative partners as family, and in a good way. On that note, we'd like to thank our families, both related and creative.

ABOUT THE AUTHOR: DAVID DANIEL

David Daniel's novel *Ark* was pulled out the slush pile at St. Martin's Press and published to wide acclaim. Since then he has published ten additional novels and more than a hundred short stories.

The Heaven Stone won a Private Eye Writers of America Award and was a Shamus Award finalist.

Among his books are *The Tuesday Man, Goofy Foot, White Rabbit, Reunion,* and two collections of short fiction: *Six Off 66* and *Coffin Dust,* all available at Amazon.com.

ABOUT THE AUTHOR: STACEY LONGO

Stacey Longo is the author of *Ordinary Boy* and *Secret Things: Twelve Tales to Terrify*. Her stories have appeared in numerous anthologies and magazines, including *Shroud*, *Shock Totem*, and the *Litchfield Literary Review*. A former humor columnist for the *Block Island Times*, she maintains a weekly humor blog at www.staceylongo.com.

Her books are available on Amazon, through her website (www.staceylongo.com) or on the Books & Boos site (http://www.booksandboos.com/new-books).

ABOUT THE AUTHOR: DALE T. PHILLIPS

Stephen King was Dale's college writing teacher, and since then Dale has published four novels, over 30 short stories, story collections, poetry, and a non-fiction career book, *How to Improve Your Interviewing Skills*.

He's appeared on stage, television, and in an independent feature film, *Throg*. He competed on two nationally televised quiz shows, *Jeopardy* and *Think Twice*, losing on both in a spectacular fashion. He co-wrote and acted in *The Nine*, a short political satire film. He's traveled to all 50 states, Mexico, Canada, and throughout Europe. Visit Dale's website at www.daletphillips.com.

ABOUT THE AUTHOR: URSULA WONG

Ursula Wong grew up on a dairy farm in central Massachusetts, and went on to become a high tech engineer. Her stories have appeared in a number of magazines including *Everyday Fiction* and *Spinetingler*.
She is a regional winner of the flash fiction contest sponsored by the New Hampshire Writer's Project (NHWP) and she leads the NHWP Nashua chapter.

Her debut novel, *Purple Trees*, concerns madness in dairy country and is available on Amazon. Visit Ursula's popular Reaching Readers Blog on her website (ursulawong.wordpress.com).

ABOUT THE AUTHOR: VLAD V.

Vlad V. is the author of *The Button, Yorick* and *Brachman's Underworld*. A freelance writer and former newspaper correspondent for the *Lowell Sun* and *Fitchburg Sentinel & Enterprise*, his work can be viewed at www.TheVlad.net.

His books are available on Amazon, Barnes & Noble, Smashwords.com, and through his website (www.TheVlad.net) or on the Books & Boos website (http://www.booksandboos.com/new-books).

Visit Books & Boos Press online at www.BooksandBoosPress.com for more great titles.

Like us on Facebook: www.facebook.com/booksandboospress

Follow us on Twitter @BooksBoosPress

Made in the USA
Charleston, SC
05 October 2014